Moving the Mountain

Charlotte Perkins Gilman

British Library Cataloguing in Publication Data

A catalogue record for this book is available from the British Library

ISBN-13: 978-1-909735-87-3

Printed and bound in Great Britain by Lightning Source UK Ltd., 6 Precedent Drive, Rooksley, Milton Keynes MK13 8PR.

Cover Illustration: *Mountains, Southern Tang Kingdom.*
Dong Yuan (circa 934 – 962)

CONTENTS

PREFACE

One of the most distinctive features of the human mind is to forecast better things.

"We look before and after
And pine for what is not."

This natural tendency to hope, desire, foresee and then, if possible, obtain, has been largely diverted from human usefulness since our goal was placed after death, in Heaven. With all our hope in "Another World," we have largely lost hope of this one.

Some minds, still keen in the perception of better human possibilities, have tried to write out their vision and give it to the world. From Plato's ideal *Republic* to Wells' *Day of the Comet* we have had many Utopias set before us, best known of which are that of Sir Thomas More and the great modern instance, *Looking Backward.*

All these have one or two distinctive features - an element of extreme remoteness, or the introduction of some mysterious outside force. *Moving the Mountain* is a short distance Utopia, a baby Utopia, a little one that can grow. It involves no other change than a change of mind, the mere awakening of people, especially the women, to existing possibilities. It indicates what people might do, real people, now living, in thirty years - if they would.

One man, truly aroused and redirecting his energies, can change his whole life in thirty years.

So can the world.

CHAPTER 1

On a gray, cold, soggy Tibetan plateau stood glaring at one another two white people - a man and a woman.

With the first, a group of peasants; with the second, the guides and carriers of a well-equipped exploring party.

The man wore the dress of a peasant, but around him was a leather belt - old, worn, battered - but a recognizable belt of no Asiatic pattern, and showing a heavy buckle made in twisted initials.

The woman's eye had caught the sunlight on this buckle before she saw that the heavily bearded face under the hood was white. She pressed forward to look at it.

"Where did you get that belt?" she cried, turning for the interpreter to urge her question.

The man had caught her voice, her words.

He threw back his hood and looked at her, with a strange blank look, as of one listening to something far away.

"John!" she cried. "John! My Brother!" He lifted a groping hand to his head, made a confused noise that ended in almost a shout of "Nellie!" reeled and fell backward.
. . . . .

When one loses his mind, as it were, for thirty years, and finds it again; when one wakes up; comes to life; recognizes oneself an American citizen twenty-five years old

No. This is what I find it so hard to realize. I am not twenty-five; I am fifty-five.
. . . . .

Well, as I was saying, when one comes to life again like this, and has to renew acquaintance with one's own mind, in a sudden swarming rush of hurrying memories - that is a good deal of pressure for a brain so long unused.

But when on top of that, one is pushed headlong into a world immeasurably different from the world one has left at twenty-five - a topsy-turvy world, wherein all one's most cherished ideals are found to be reversed, rearranged, or utterly gone; where strange new facts are accompanied by strange new thoughts and strange new feelings - the pressure becomes terrific,

Nellie has suggested that I write it down, and I think for once she is right. I disagree with her on so many points that I am glad to recognize the wisdom of this idea. It will certainly be a useful process in my re-education; and relieve the mental tension.

So, to begin with my first life, being now in my third

. . . . .

I am the only son of a Methodist minister of South Carolina. My mother was a Yankee. She died after my sister Ellen was born, when I was seven years old. My father educated me well. I was sent to a small Southern college, and showed such a talent for philology that I specialized in ancient languages, and, after some teaching and the taking of various degrees, I had a

[*Two pages are missing here.* (ed.)]

they never mentioned such a detail. Furthermore, they gave so dim an account of where the place was that we don't know now; should have to locate that night's encampment, and then look for a precipice and go down it with ropes.

As I have no longer any interest in those venerable races and time-honored customs, I think we will not do this.

Well, she found me, and something happened. She says I knew her - shouted "Nellie!" and fell down - fell on a stone, too, and hit my head so hard they thought I was dead this time "for sure." But when I "came to" I came all the way, back to where I was thirty years ago; and as for those thirty years - I do not remember one day of them.

Nor do I wish to. I have those filthy Tibetan clothes, sterilized and packed away, but I never want to look at them.

I am back in the real world, back where I was at twenty-five. But now I am fifty-five —

. . . . .

Now, about Nellie. I must go slowly and get this thing straightened out for good and all.

My little sister! I was always fond of her, and she adored me. She looked up to me, naturally; believed everything I told her; minded me like a little dog - when she was a child. And as she grew into girl-hood, I had a strong restraining influence upon her. She wanted to be educated - to go to college - but father wouldn't hear of it, of course, and I backed him up. If there is anything on earth I always hated and despised, it is a strong-minded woman! That is - it *was*. I certainly cannot hate and despise my sister Nellie.

Now it appears that soon after my departure from this life father died, very suddenly. Nellie inherited the farm - and the farm turned out to be a mine, and the mine turned out to be worth a good deal of money.

So that poor child, having no natural guardian or protector, just set to work for herself - went to college to her heart's content, to a foreign university, too. She studied medicine, practiced a while, then was offered a chair in a college and took it; then - I hate to write it - but she is now president of a college - *a co-educational college!*

"Don't you mean 'dean?'" I asked her.

"No," she said. "There is a dean of the girl's building - but I am the president."

My little sister!

. . . . .

The worst of it is that my little sister is now forty-eight, and I— to all intents and purposes - am twenty-five! She is twenty-three years older than I am. She has had thirty years of world-life which I have missed entirely, and this thirty years, I begin to gather, has covered more changes than an ordinary century or two.

It is lucky about that mine.

"At least I shall not have to worry about money," I said to her when she told me about our increased fortune.

She gave one of those queer little smiles, as if she had something up her sleeve, and said:

"No; you won't have to worry in the least about money."

Having all that medical skill of hers in the background, she took excellent care of me up there on those dreary plains and hills, brought me back to the coast by easy stages, and home on one of those new steamers - but I mustn't stop to describe the details of each new thing I notice!

I have sense enough myself, even if I'm not a doctor, to use my mind gradually, not to swallow too fast, as it were.

Nellie is a little inclined to manage me. I don't know as I blame her. I do feel like a child, sometimes. It is so humiliating not to know little common things such as everybody else knows. Air ships I expected, of course; they had started before I left. They are common enough, all sizes. But water is still the cheaper route - as well as slower.

Nellie said she didn't want me to get home too quick; she wanted time to explain things. So we spent long, quiet hours in our steamer chairs, talking things over.

It's no use asking about the family; there is only a flock of young cousins and "once removed" now; the aunts and uncles are mostly gone. Uncle Jake is left. Nellie grins wickedly when she mentions him.

"If things get too hard on you, John, you can go down to Uncle Jake's and rest up. He and Aunt Dorcas haven't moved an *inch*. They fairly barricade their minds against a new idea - and he ploughs and she cooks up on that little mountain farm just as they always did. People go to see them "

"Why shouldn't they?" I asked. And she smiled that queer little smile again.

"I mean they go to see them as if they were the Pyramids."

"I see," said I. "I might as well prepare for some preposterous nightmare of a world, like - what was that book of Wells', 'The Sleeper Awakened?' "

"Oh, yes; I remember that book," she answered, "and a lot of others. People were already guessing about things as they might be, weren't they? But what never struck any of them was that the people themselves could change."

"No," I agreed. "You can't alter human nature."

Nellie laughed - laughed out loud. Then she squeezed my hand and patted it.

"You *Dear*! she said. "You precious old Long–Lost Brother! When you get too utterly upset I'll wear my hair down, put on a short dress and let you boss me awhile - to keep your spirits up. That was just the phrase, wasn't it? - 'You can't alter human nature!' " And she laughed again.

There is something queer about Nellie - very queer. It is not only that she is different from my little sister - that's natural; but she is different from any woman of forty-eight I ever saw - from any woman of any age I ever saw.

In the first place, she doesn't look *old* - not at all. Women of forty, in our region, were *old women*, and Nellie's near fifty! Then she isn't - what shall I call it - dependent; not the least in the world. As soon as I became really conscious, and strong enough to be of any use, and began to offer her those little services and attentions due to a woman, I noticed this difference.

She is brisk, firm, assured - not unpleasantly so; I don't mean a thing of that sort; but somehow like - almost like a man! No, I certainly don't mean that. She is not in the least mannish, nor in the least self-assertive; but she takes things so easily - as if she owned them.

I suppose it will be some time before my head is absolutely clear and strong as it used to be. I tire rather easily. Nellie is very reassuring about it. She says it will take about a year to re-establish connections and renew mental processes. She advises me to read and talk only a little every day, to sleep all I can, and not to worry.

"You'll be all right soon, my dear," she says, "and plenty of life before you. You seem to have led a very healthy out-door life. You're really well and strong - and as good-looking as ever."

At least she hasn't forgotten that woman's chief duty is to please.

"And the world is a much better place to be in than it was," she assured me. "Things will surprise you, of course - things I have gotten used to and shall forget to tell you about. But the changes are all good ones, and you'll soon get - acclimated. You're young yet."

That's where Nellie slips up. She cannot help having me in mind as the brave young brother she knew. She forgets that I am an old man now. Finally I told her that.

"No, John Robertson," she she, "that's where you are utterly wrong. Of course, you don't know what we're doing about age - how differently we feel. As a matter of physiology we find that about one hundred and fifty ought to be our natural limit; and that with proper conditions we can easily get to be a hundred now. Ever so many do."

"I don't want to be a hundred," I protested. "I saw a man of ninety-eight once, and never want to be one."

"It's not like that now," she said. "I mean we live to be a hundred and enjoy life still - 'keep our faculties,' as they used to put it. Why, the ship's doctor here is eighty-seven."

This surprised me a good deal. I had talked a little with this man, and had thought him about sixty.

"Then a man of a hundred, according to your story, would look like - like ..."

"Like Grandpa Ely," she offered.

I remembered my mother's father - a tall, straight, hale old man of seventy-five. He had a clear eye, a firm step, a rosy color in his face. Well, that wasn't so bad a prospect.

"I consent to be a hundred - on those terms," I told her.

. . . . .

She talked to me a good bit, in small daily doses, of the more general changes in the world, showed me new maps, even let me read a little in the current magazines.

"I suppose you have a million of these now," I said. "There were thousands when I left!"

"No," she answered. "There are fewer, I believe; but much better."

I turned over the one in my hand. It was pleasantly light and thin, it opened easily, the paper and presswork were of the best, the price was twenty-five cents.

"Is this a cheap one - at a higher price? or have the best ones come down?"

"It's a cheap one," she told me, "if you mean by that a popular one, and it's cheap enough. They have all of a million subscribers."

"And what's the difference, beyond the paper and print?" I asked.

"The pictures are good."

I looked it through again.

"Yes, very good, much improved. But I don't see anything phenomenal - unless it is the absence of advertisements."

Nellie took it out of my hand and ran it over.

"Just read some of that," she said. "Read this story - and this article - and that."

So I sat reading in the sunny silence, the gulls wheeling and dipping just as they used to, and the wide purple ocean just as changeable - and changeless - as ever.

One of the articles was on an extension of municipal service, and involved so much comment on preceding steps that I found it most enlightening. The other was a recent suggestion in educational psychology, and this too carried a retrospect of recent progress which gave me food for thought. The story was a clever one. I found it really amusing, and only on a second reading did I find what it was that gave the queer flavor to it. It was a story about women - two women who were in business partnership, with their adventures, singly and together.

I looked through it carefully. They were not even girls, they were not handsome, they were not in process of being married - in fact, it was not once mentioned whether they were married or not, ever had been or ever wanted to be. Yet I had found it amusing!

I laid the magazine on my rug-bound knees and meditated. A queer sick feeling came over me - mental, not physical. I looked through the magazine again. It was not what I should have called "a woman's magazine," yet the editor was a woman, most of the contributors were women, and in all the subject matter I began to detect allusions and references of tremendous import.

Presently Nellie came to see how I was getting on. I saw her approaching, a firm, brisk figure, well and becomingly dressed, with a tailored trimness and convenience, far indeed from the slim, graceful, yielding girl I had once been so proud to protect and teach.

"How soon do we get in, Lady Manager?" I asked her.

"Day after tomorrow," she answered back promptly - not a word about going to see, or asking anyone!

"Well, ma'am, I want you to sit down here and tell me things - right now. What am I to expect? Are there *no* men left in America?"

She laughed gaily.

"No men! Why, bless you, there are as many men as there are women, and a few more, I believe. Not such an over-plus as there used to be, but some to spare still. We had a million and a half extra in your day, you know."

"I'm glad to learn we're allowed to live!" said I. "Now tell me the worst - are the men all doing the housework?"

"You call that 'the worst,' do you?" inquired Nellie, cocking her head to one side and looking at me affectionately, and yet quizzically. "Well, I guess it was - pretty near 'the worst!' No dear, men are doing just as many kinds of business as they ever were."

I heaved a sigh of relief and chucked my magazine under the chair.

"I'd begun to think there weren't any men left. And they still wear trousers, don't they?"

She laughed outright.

"Oh, yes. They wear just as many trousers as they did before."

"And what do the women wear," I demanded suspiciously.

"Whatever kind of clothing their work demands," she answered.

"Their work? What kind of work do they do?"

"All kinds - anything they like."

I groaned and shut my eyes. I could see the world as I left it, with only a small proportion of malcontents and a large majority of contented and happy homes; and then I saw this awful place I was coming to, with strange, masculine women and subdued men.

"How does it happen that there aren't any on this ship?" I inquired.

"Any what?" asked Nellie.

"Any of these - New Women?"

"Why, there are. They're all new, except Mrs. Talbot. She's older than I am, and rather reactionary."

This Mrs. Talbot was a stiff, pious, narrow-minded old lady, and I had liked her the least of any on board.

"Do you mean to tell me that pretty Mrs. Exeter is - one of this new kind?"

"Mrs. Exeter owns - and manages - a large store, if that is what you mean."

"And those pretty Borden girls?"

"They do house decorating - have been abroad on business."

"And Mrs. Green - and Miss Sandwich?"

"One of them is a hat designer, one a teacher. This is toward the end of vacation, and they're all coming home, you see."

"And Miss Elwell?"

Miss Elwell was quite the prettiest woman on board, and seemed to have plenty of attention - just like the girls I remembered.

"Miss Elwell is a civil engineer," said my sister.

"It's horrid," I said. "It's perfectly horrid! And aren't there any women left?"

"There's Aunt Dorcas," said Nellie, mischievously, "and Cousin Drusilla. You remember Drusilla?"

CHAPTER 2

The day after tomorrow! I was to see it the day after tomorrow - this strange, new, abhorrent world!

The more I considered what bits of information I had gleaned already, the more I disliked what lay before me. In the first blazing light of returned memory and knowledge, the first joy of meeting my sister, the hope of seeing home again, I had not distinguished very sharply between what was new to my bewildered condition and what was new indeed - new to the world as well as to me. But now a queer feeling of disproportion and unreality began to haunt me.

As my head cleared, and such knowledge as I was now gathering began to help towards some sense of perspective and relation, even my immediate surroundings began to assume a sinister importance.

Any change, to any person, is something of a shock, though sometimes a beneficial one. Changes too sudden, and too great, are hard to bear, for any one. But who can understand the peculiar horror of my unparalleled experience?

Slowly the thing took shape in my mind.

There was the first, irrevocable loss - my life!

Thirty years - *the* thirty years in which a man may really live - these were gone from me forever.

I was coming back; strong to be sure; well enough in health; even, I hoped, with my old mental vigor - *but not to the same world.*

Even the convict who survives thirty years imprisonment, may return at length to the same kind of world he had left so long.

But I! It was as if I had slept, and, in my sleep, they had stolen my world.

I threw off the thought, and started in to action.

Here was a small world - the big steamer beneath me. I had already learned much about her. In the first place, she was not a"steamer," but a thing for which I had no name; her power was electric,

"Oh, well," I thought, as I examined her machinery, "this I might have expected. Thirty years of such advances as we were making in 1910 were sure to develop electric motors of all sorts."

The engineer was a pleasant, gentlemanly fellow, more than willing to talk about his profession and its marvellous advances. The ship was well manned, certainly; though the work required was far less than it used to be, the crew were about as numerous. I had made some acquaintances among the ship's officers - even among the men, who were astonishingly civil and well-mannered - but I had not at first noticed the many points of novelty in their attitude or in my surroundings.

Now I paced the deck and considered the facts I had observed - the perfect ventilation of the vessel, the absence of the smell of cooking and of bilge water, the dainty convenience and appropriate beauty of all the fittings and furnishings, the smooth speed and steadiness of her,

The quarters of the crew I found as remarkable as anything else about the vessel; indeed the forecastle and steerage differed more from what I remembered than from any other part. Every person on board had a clean and comfortable lodging, though there were grades of distinction in size and decoration. But any gentleman could have lived in that "foks'le" without discomfort. Indeed, I soon found that many gentlemen did. I discovered, quite by accident, that one of the crew was a Harvard man. He was not at all loath to talk of it, either - was evidently no black sheep of any sort.

Why had he chosen this work?

Oh, he wanted the experience - it widened life, knowing different trades.

Why was he not an officer then?

He didn't care to work at it long enough - this was only experience work, you see.

I did not see, nor ask, but I inferred, and it gave me again that feeling as if the ground underfoot had wiggled slightly.

Was that old dream of Bellamy's stalking abroad? Were young men portioned out to menial service, willy-nilly?

It was evidently not a universal custom, for some of the sailors were much older men, and long used to the business. I got hold of one who seemed more like the deckhands of old days, though cleaner and more cheerful; a man who was all of sixty.

Yes he had followed the sea from boyhood. Yes, he liked it, always had liked it, liked it better now than when he was young.

He had seen many changes? I listened carefully, though I asked the question lightly enough.

Changes! He guessed he had. Terbacca was better for one thing - I was relieved to see that men still smoked, and then the jar came again as I remembered that save for this man, and one elderly officer, I had not seen anyone smoking on the vessel.

"How do you account for it?" I asked the old Yankee. "For tobacco's being better?"

He grinned cheerfully. "Less run on it, I guess," said he. "Young fellers don't seem to smoke no more, and I ain't seen nobody chewing for - well, for ten years back."

"Is it cheaper as well as better?"

"No, sir, it ain't. It's perishing high. But then, wages is high, too," he grudgingly admitted.

"Better tobacco and better wages - anything else improved?"

"Yes, sir-ee! Grub's better, by square miles - and 'commodations - an' close. Make better stuff now."

"Well! well!" said I as genially as I knew how. "That's very different from my young days. Then everybody older than I always complained about all manner of things, and told how much better - and cheaper - things were when they were young."

"Yes, 'twas so," he admitted meditatively. "But 'tain't so now. Shoes is better, most things is better, I guess. Seems like water runnin' up hill, don't it, sir?"

It did. I didn't like it. I got away from the old man, and walked by myself - like Kipling's cat.

"Of course, of course!" I said to myself impatiently, "I may as well expect to find everything as much improved from what it was in my time as in, say, sixty years before.

That sort of progress goes faster and faster. Things change, but people - "

And here is where I got this creepy sense of unreality.

At first everything was so strange to me, and my sister was so kind and thoughtful, so exquisitely considerate of my feelings and condition, that I had failed to notice this remarkable circumstance - so were the other people. It was like being in a - well, in a house-party of very nice persons. Kind, cheerful, polite - here I suddenly realized that I had not seen a grouchy face, heard an unkind remark, felt, as one does feel through silk and broadcloth, the sense of discontent and disapproval.

There was one, the somewhat hard-faced old lady, Mrs. Talbot, of whom I had hopes. I sought her, and laid myself out to please her by those little attentions which are so grateful to an elderly woman from a young man.

Her accepting these as a commonplace, her somewhat too specific inquiries about my health, suddenly reminded me that I was not a young man.

She talked on while I made again that effort at readjustment which was so hideously hard. Gone in a night - all my young manhood - gone untasted!

"Do you find it difficult to concentrate your attention?" she was saying, a steely eye fixed upon my face.

"I beg your pardon, madam. I fear I do. You were saying - "

"I was saying that you will find many changes when you get back."

"I find them already, Mrs. Talbot. They rather loom up. It *is* sudden, you see."

"Yes, you've been away a long time, I understand. In the far East?"

Mrs. Talbot was the first person who had asked me a question. Evidently hers were the manners of an older generation, and for once I had to admit that the younger generation had improved.

But I recalled the old defensive armor against the old assaults.

"Quite a while," I answered cheerfully, "Quite a while. Now what should you think would impress me most - in the way of change?"

"The women," she answered promptly.

I smiled my gallantest, and replied, bowing:

"I find them still charming."

Her set face broke into a pleased smile.

"You do my heart good!" she cried. "I haven't heard a compliment in fifteen years."

"Good Heavens, madam! what are our men thinking of?"

"It's not the men's fault; it's the women's. They won't have it."

"Are there many of these - new women?"

"There's nothing else - except a few old ones like me."

I hastened to assure her that a woman like her would never be called old - and she looked as pleased as a girl.

Presently I excused myself and left her, with relief. It was annoying beyond measure to have the only specimen of the kind of woman I used to like turn out to be personally the kind I never liked.

On the opposite deck, I found Miss Elwell - and for once alone. A retiring back, wearing an aggrieved expression showed that it had not been for long.

"May I join you, Miss Elwell?"

I might. I did. We paced up and down, silent for a bit.

She was a joy to the eye, a lovely, straight, young thing, with a fresh, pure color and eyes of dancing brightness. I spoke of this and that aboard ship - the sea, the weather; and she was so gaily friendly, so sweet and modest, yet wholly frank, that I grew quite happy in her company.

My sister must have been mistaken about her being a civil engineer. She might be a college girl - but nothing worse. And she was so pretty!

I devoted myself to Miss Elwell 'till she took herself off, probably to join her - her - it occurred to me that I had seen no one with Miss Elwell.

"Nellie" said I, "for heaven's sake give me the straight of all this. I'm going distracted with the confusion. What has happened to the world? Tell me all, I can bear it - as the extinct novels used to say. But I cannot bear this terrible suspense! Don't you have novels any more?"

"Novels? Oh, yes, plenty; better than ever were written. You'll find it splendidly worth while to read quite a few of them while you're getting oriented . . . Well, you want a kind of running, historic sketch?"

"Yes. Give me the outlines - just the heads, as it were. You see, my dear, it is not easy to get readjusted even to the old things, and there are so many new ones "

We were in our steamer chairs, most people dozing after their midday meal. She reached over and took my hand in hers, and held it tight. It was marvelously comforting, this one live visible link between what was forever past and this uncertain future. But for her, even those old, old days might have flickered and seemed doubtful - I should have felt like one swimming under water and not knowing, which way was up. She gave me solid ground underfoot at any rate. Whatever her place might be in this New World, she had talked to me only of the old one.

In these long, quiet, restful days, she had revived in my mind the pleasant memories of our childhood together; our little Southern home; our patient, restrained Northern mother and the fine education she gave her school-less little ones; our high-minded - and, alas, narrow-minded - father, handsome, courteous, inflexible. Under Nellie's gentle leading, my long unused memory-cells had revived like rain-washed leaves, and my past life had, at last, grown clear and steady.

My college life; my old chum, Granger, who had visited us once; our neighbors and relations; little gold-haired Cousin Drusilla, whom I, in ten years proud seniority, had teased as a baby, played with and tyrannized over as a confiding child, and kissed good-bye - a slim, startled little figure - when I left for Asia.

Nellie had always spoken of things as I remembered them, and avoided adroitly, or quietly refused to discuss, their new aspects.

I think she was right - at first.

"Out with it!" said I. "Come - Have we adopted Socialism?" I braced myself for the answer.

"Socialism? Oh - why, yes. I think we did. But that was twenty years ago."

"And it didn't last? You've proved the impracticable folly of it? You've discarded it?"

I sat up straight, very eager.

"Why, no - " said Nellie. "It's very hard to put these new things into old words - We've got beyond it."

"Beyond Socialism! Not - not - Anarchy?"

"Oh, bless you, no; no indeed! We understand better what socialism meant, that's all. We have more, much more, than it ever asked; but we don't call it that."

I did not understand.

"It's like this," she said. "Suppose you had left a friend in the throes of a long, tempestuous' courtship, full of ardor, of keen joy, and keener anticipation. Then, returning, you say to your friend, 'Do you still have courtship?' And he says, 'Why no, I'm married.' It's not that he has discarded it, proved it's impracticable folly. He had to have it - he liked it - but he's got beyond it."

"Go on and elucidate," I said. "I don't quite follow your parable."

She considered a bit.

"Well, here's a more direct parallel. Back in the 18th century, the world was wild about Democracy - Democracy was going to do all things for all men. Then, with prodigious struggles, they acquired some Democracy - set it going. It was a good thing. But it took time. It grew. It had difficulties. In the next century, there was less talk about all the heavenly results of Democracy, and more definite efforts to make it work."

This was clearer.

"You mean," I followed her slowly.

"That what was called socialism was attained - and you've been improving upon it?"

"Exactly, Brother, 'you are on' - as we used to say. But even that's not the main step."

"No? What else?"

"Only a New Religion."

I showed my disappointment. Nellie watched my face silently. She laughed. She even kissed me.

"John" said she, "I could make vast sums by exhibiting you to psychologists! as An Extinct Species of Mind. You'd draw better than a Woolly Mammoth."

I smiled wryly; and she squeezed my hand. "Might as well make a joke of it, Old Man - you've got to get used to it, and 'the sooner the quicker!' "

"All right - Go ahead with your New Religion."

She sat back in her chair with an expression of amused retrospection.

"I had forgotten," she said, "I had really forgotten. We didn't use to think much of religion, did we?"

"Father did," said I.

"No, not even Father and his kind - they only used it as a - what was the old joke? a patent fire escape! Nobody appreciated Religion!"

"They spent much time and money on it," I suggested.

"*That's* not appreciation!"

"Well, come on with the story. Did you have another Incarnation of any body?"

"You might call it that," Nellie allowed, her voice growing quietly earnest, "We certainly had somebody with an unmistakable Power."

This did not interest me at all. I hated to see Nellie looking so sweetly solemn over her "New Religion," In the not unnatural reaction of a minister's son, rigidly reared, I had had small use for religion of any sort. As a scholar I had studied them all, and felt as little reverence for the ancient ones as for the shifty mushroom crop of new sects and schools of thought with which the country teemed in my time.

"Now, look here, John," said she at length, "I've been watching you pretty closely and I think you're equal to a considerable mental effort - In one way, it may be easier for you, just because you've not seen a bit of it - anyhow, you've got to face it. Our world has changed in these thirty years, more than the change between what it used to be and what people used to imagine about Heaven. Here is the first thing you've got to do - mentally. You must understand, clearly, in your human consciousness, that the objection and distaste you feel is only in your personal consciousness. Everything is better; there is far more comfort, pleasure, peace of mind; a richer swifter growth, a higher happier life in every way; and yet, you won't like it because your - " she seemed to hesitate for a word, now and then; as one trying to translate, "reactions are all tuned to earlier conditions. If you can understand this and see over your own personal - attitudes - it will not be long before a real convincing *sense* of joy, of life, will follow the intellectual perception that things are better."

"Hold on," I said, "Let me chew on that a little."

"As if," I presently suggested, "as if I'd left a home that was poor and dirty and crowded, with a pair of quarrelsome inefficient parents - drunken and abusive, maybe, and a lot of horrid, wrangling, selfish, little brothers and sisters - and woke up one fine morning in a great clean beautiful house - richly furnished - full of a lot of angels - who were total strangers?"

"Exactly!" she cried. "Hurrah for you, Johnnie, you couldn't have defined it better."

"I don't like it," said I. "I'd rather have my old home and my own family than all the princely palaces and amiable angels you could dream of in a hundred years."

"Mother had an old story-book by a New England author," Nellie quietly remarked, "where somebody said, 'You can't always have your "druthers" ' - she used to quote it to me when I was little and complained that things were not as I wanted them. - "John, dear, please remember that the new people in the new world find it 'like home' and love it far better than we used to. It'll be queer to you, but it's a pleasant commonplace to them. We have found out at last that it is natural to be happy."

She was silent and I was silent; till I asked her "What's the name of your new religion?"

"It hasn't any," she answered.

"Hasn't any? What do they call it? the Believers, I mean?"

"They call it 'Living' and 'Life' - that's all."

"Hm! and what's their specialty?"

Nellie gave a funny little laugh, part sad, part tender, part amused.

"I had no idea it would be so hard to tell you things," she said. "You'll have to just see for yourself, I guess."

"Do go on, Nellie. I'll be good. You were going to tell me, in a nutshell, what had happened - please do."

"The thing that has happened," said she, slowly, "is just this. The world has come alive. We are doing in a pleasant, practical way, all the things which we could have done, at any time before - only we never thought so. The real change is this: we have changed our minds. This happened very soon after you left. Ah! that was a time! To think that you should have missed it!" She gave my hand another sympathetic squeeze and went on. "After that it was only a question of time, of how soon we could do things. And we've been doing them ever since, faster and faster."

This seemed rather flat and disappointing.

"I don't see that you make out anything wonderful - so far. A new Religion which seems to consist only in behaving better; and a gradual improvement of social conditions - all that was going on when I left."

Nellie regarded me with a considering eye.

"I see how you interpret it," she said, "behaving better in our early days was a small personal affair; either a pathetically inadequate failure to do what one could not, or a pharisaic, self-righteous success in doing what one could. All personal - personal!"

"Good behavior has to be a personal affair, hasn't it?" I mildly protested.

"Not by any means!" said Nellie with decision. "That was precisely what kept us so small and bad, so miserably confined and discouraged. Like a lot of well-meaning soldiers imagining that their evolutions were 'a personal affair' - or an orchestra plaintively protesting that if each man played a correct tune of his own choosing, the result would be perfect! Dear! dear! No, *Sir*" she continued with some fierceness, "that's just where we changed our minds! Humanity has come alive, I tell you and we have reason to be proud of our race!"

She held her head high, there was a glad triumphant look in her eyes - not in the least religious. Said she: "You'll see results. That will make it clearer to you than anything I can say. But if I may remark that we have no longer the fear of death - much less of damnation, and no such thing as 'sin'; that the only kind of prison left is called a quarantine - that punishment is unknown but preventive means are of a drastic and sweeping nature such as we never dared think of before - that there is no such thing in the civilized world as poverty - no labor problem - no color problem - no sex problem - almost no disease - very little accident - practically no fires - that the world is rapidly being reforested - the soil improved; the output growing in quantity and quality; that no one needs to work over two hours a day and most people work four - that we have no graft - no adulteration of goods - no malpractice - no crime."

"Nellie," said I, "you are a woman and my sister. I'm very sorry, but I don't believe it."

"I thought you wouldn't," said she. Women always will have the last word.

CHAPTER 3

The blue shore line of one's own land always brings a thrill of the heart; to me, buried exile as I had been, the heart-leap was choking.

Ours was a slow steamer, and we did not stop at Montauk where the mail and the swiftest travelers landed, nor in Jamaica Harbor with the immigrants.

As we swept along the sunny, level spaces of the South shore, Nellie told me how Long Island was now the "Reception Room" of our country, instead of poor, brutal little Ellis Island.

"The shores are still mostly summer places," she said. "One of the most convincing of our early lines of advance was started on the South shore; and there are plenty of Country Clubs, Home Parks and things like that; but the bulk of the island toward the western end is an experiment station in applied sociology.

I was watching the bright shore hungrily. With a glass I could see many large buildings, not too closely set.

"I should think it would spoil the place for homes," I said.

Nellie had a way of listening to my remarks, kindly and pleasantly, but as if I were somehow a long way off and she was trying to grasp what I said.

"In a way it did - at first;" she explained presently, "but even then it meant just as many homes for other people, and now it means so much more!"

She hesitated a moment and then plunged in resolutely.

"You're in for a steady course of instructive remarks from now on. Everybody will be explaining things and bragging about them. We haven't outgrown some of the smaller vices, you see. As to this 'Immigration Problem' - we woke up to this fact among others, that the 'reintegration of peoples' as Ward called it, was a sociological process not possible to stop, but quite possible to assist and to guide to great advantage. And here in America we recognized our own special place - "the melting pot you know?"

Yes, I remembered the phrase, I never liked it. Our family were pure English stock, and rightly proud of their descent.

"I begin to see, my dear sister, that while receiving the torrent of instructive remarks you foretell, the way of wisdom for me is steadfastly to withhold my own opinions."

Nellie laughed appreciatively.

"You always had a long head, John. Well, whether you like it or not, our people saw their place and power at last and rose to it. We refuse no one. We have discovered as many ways of utilizing human waste as we used to have for the waste products of coal tar."

"You don't mean to say idiots and criminals?" I protested.

"Idiots, hopeless ones, we don't keep any more," she answered gently. "They are very rare now. The grade of average humanity is steadily rising; and we have the proud satisfaction of knowing we have helped it rise. We organized a permanent 'reception committee' for the whole country, one station here and one in California. Anybody could come - but they had to submit to our handling when they did come."

"We used to have physical examination, didn't we?"

"A rudimentary one. What we have now is Compulsory Socialization."

I stared at her.

"Yes, I know! You are thinking of that geological kind of evolution people used to talk about, and 'you can't alter human nature.' In the first place, we can. In the second place, we do. In the third place, there isn't so much alteration needed as we used to think. Human nature is a pretty good thing. No immigrant is turned loose on the community till he or she is up to a certain standard, and the children we educate."

"We always did, didn't we?"

"Always did? Why brother, we didn't know what the word meant in your time."

"I shall be glad to follow that up," I assured her. "Education was improving even in the old days, I remember. I shall be glad to see the schools."

"Some of them you won't know when you do see them," said Nellie. "On Long Island we have agricultural and industrial stations like - like - I think we had something like it in some of our Western colleges, which it was the fashion to look down upon. We have a graded series of dwellings where the use of modern conveniences is taught to all newcomers."

"Suppose they won't learn? They used to prefer to live like hogs, as I remember."

Again Nellie looked at me as if I were speaking to her from a distance.

"We used to say so - and I suppose we used to think so - some of us. But we know better now. These people are not compelled to come to our country, but if they come they know what they have to do - and they do it. You may have noticed that we have no 'steerage'."

I had noticed it.

"They have decent surroundings from the first step. They have to be antiseptically clean, they and all their belongings, before entering the ship."

"But what an awful expense!" I ventured.

"Suppose you keep cattle, John, and knew how to fatten and improve them; and suppose your ranch was surrounded by strays - mavericks - anxious to come in. Would you call it 'an expense' to add to your herd?"

"You can't sell people."

"No, but you can profit by their labor."

"That sounds like the same old game. I should think your Socialism would have put an end to that."

"Socialism did not alter the fact that wealth comes by labor," she replied. "All these people work. We provide the opportunity for them, we train them to higher efficiency, especially the children. The very best and wisest of us are proud to serve there - as women used to be proud when they were invited 'to help receive' some personage. We receive Humanity - and introduce it to America. What they produce is used to cover the expense of their training, and also to lay up a surplus for themselves."

"They must produce more than they used to," observed I drily.

"They do," said Nellie.

"You might as well finish this thing up," I said. "Then when people talk to me about immigration, I can look intelligent and say, 'I know about that.' And really, I'm interested. How do you begin with 'em?"

"When they come into Jamaica Harbor they see a great crescent of white piers, each with its gate. We'll go and see it some day - splendid arches with figures on them, like the ones they used to put up for Triumphs. There's the German Gate and the Spanish Gate, the English Gate, the Italian Gate - and so on. There is welcome in their own language - and instruction in ours. There is physical examination - the most searching and thorough - microscopic - chemical. They have to come up to a certain standard before they are graduated, you see."

"Graduated?"

"Yes. We have a standard of citizenship now - an idea of what people ought to be and how to make them so. Dear me! To think that you don't know about that - "

"I shouldn't think they'd stand for it - all this examination and so on."

"No country on earth offers so much happiness to its people. Nowhere else - yet - is there as good opportunity to be helped up, to have real scientific care, real loving study and assistance! Everybody likes to be made the most of! Everybody - nearly - has the feeling that they might be something better if they had a chance! We give them the chance."

"Then I should think you'd have all creation on your hands at once."

"And depopulate the other nations? They had something to say about that! You see this worked all sorts of ways. In the first place, when we got all the worst and lowest people, that left an average of better ones at home - people who could learn more quickly. When we proved what good stuff human nature was, rightly treated, they all took heart of grace and began to improve their own. Then, as our superior attractions steadily drew off 'the lower classes,' that raised the value of those who remained. They were better paid, better thought of at home. As more and more people came to us, the other nations got rather alarmed, and began to establish counter attractions - to keep their folks at home. Also, many other nations had some better things than we did, you remember. And finally most people love their own country better than any other, no matter how good. No, the balance of population is not seriously altered."

"Still, with such an influx of low-grade people you must have a Malthusian torrent of increasing population on your hands."

Again that odd listening look, her head a little on one side.

"I have to keep remembering," she said. "Have to recall what people wrote and said and thought in the past generation. The idea was that people had to increase like rabbits, and would eat up the food supply, so wars and pestilences and all manner of cruel conditions were necessary to 'keep down the population.' Wasn't that it?"

"You are twenty years out, my dear!" I rejoiced to assure her. "We had largely passed that, and were beginning to worry about the decreasing birth rate - among the more intelligent. It was only the lowest grade that kept on 'like rabbits' as you say. But it's that sort you seem to have been filling in with. I should think it would have materially lowered the average. Or have you, in this new 'forcing system' made decent people out of scrubs?"

"That's exactly what we've done; we've improved the people and lowered the birth-rate at one stroke!"

"They were beginning to talk eugenics when I left."

"This is not eugenics - we have made great advances in that, of course; but the chief factor in this change is a common biological law - 'individuation is in inverse proportion to reproduction,' you know. We individualize the women - develop their personal power, their human characteristics - and they don't have so many children."

"I don't see how that helps unless you have eliminated the brutality of men."

"My dear brother, the brutality of men *lowered* the birthrate - it didn't raise it! One of those undifferentiated peasant women would have a baby every year if she was married to a saint - and she couldn't have more in polyandry - unless it were twins! No, the birthrate was for women to settle - and they have."

"Out of fashion to have children at all?"

"No, John, you needn't sneer. We have better children than ever were born on earth before, and they grade higher every year. But we are approaching a balanced population."

I didn't like the subject, and turned to the clear skyline of the distant city. It towered as of old, but seemed not so close-packed. Not one black cloud - and very few white ones!

"You've ended the smoke nuisance, I'm glad to see. Has steam gone, too?"

"We use electricity altogether in all the cities now," she said. "It occurred to us that to pipe a leaking death into every bedroom; to thread the city with poison, fire and explosion, was foolish."

"Defective wiring used to cause both death and conflagration, didn't it?"

"It did," she admitted; "but it is not 'defective' any more."

"Is the coal all gone?"

"No, but we burn it at the mines - by a process which does *not* waste ninety per cent of the energy - and transmit the power."

"For all New York?"

"Oh, no. New York has enough water power, you see. The tide mills are enough for this whole region."

"They solved the tide-mill problem, did they?"

"Yes. There are innumerable mechanical advances, of course. You'll enjoy them."

We were near enough now to see the city clearly.

"What a splendid water front!" I cried. "Why, this is glorious."

It surely was. The wide shores swung away, glittering in the pure sunlight. Staten Island lay behind us, a vision of terraced loveliness; the Jersey shore shone clear, no foul pall of oil smoke overhanging; the Brooklyn banks were banks of palaces, and Manhattan itself towered royally before us, all bordered with broad granite piers.

"'Marginal mile after mile of smooth-running granite embankment'" quoted Nellie. "'Broad steps of marble descending for the people to enter the water. White-pillared piers '"

"Look at the water!" I cried, suddenly. "It's clear!"

"Of course it's clear," she agreed laughingly. "This is a civilized country, I tell you."

I looked and looked. It was blue and bright in the distance; it was a clear, soft green beneath us. I saw a fish leap.

"So far I'm with you, anyhow," said I. "That certainly is a big step - and looks like a miracle. New York harbor *clean*! . . . How about customs?" I asked as we drew in.

"Gone - clean forgotten - with a lot of other foolishness. The air ships settled that. We couldn't plant custom houses in the air, you see - along ten thousand miles of coast and border."

I was watching the shore. There were plenty of people about, but strangely gay of aspect and bright-colored in raiment. I could see amusement piers - numbers of them - some evidently used as gymnasia, in some there was dancing. Motor cars of all descriptions ran swiftly and quietly about. Air ships, large and small, floated off, to the north and west mostly. The water was freckled with pleasure boats. I heard singing - and music.

"Some new holiday?" I ventured.

"Not at all," said my sister. "It is afternoon."

She watched me, quizzically.

"It is afternoon," she repeated. "Let that sink in!"

It sank in, slowly.

"Do you mean that no one works in the afternoon?"

"No one - except those who don't work in the morning. Some kinds of work can't stop, of course; but most kinds can. I told you before - no one *has* to work more than two hours a day; most people work four. Why?" She saw my unbelieving stare. "Because we like to. Also because we are ambitious," she went on. "I told you of the gain we've made in 'the civilized world.' Not all of it is civilized. We are still missionarying. And while there is need of help anywhere on earth, most of us work overtime. Also it lays up public capital - we are planning some vast undertakings - and gives a wider margin for vacations."

I was thinking in a hazy way of a world that was not tired, not driven, no nose on any grindstone; of a people who only had to work two hours - and worked four! Yet there was every evidence of increased wealth.

Suddenly Nellie gave a joyous little cry.

"Why, there's Owen!" she waved her veil. "And there's Jerrold and Hallier. She fairly danced with pleasure.

I could see a big grayish man madly waving his hat down there - and two young folks hopping up and down and flourishing handkerchiefs, among many similarly excited.

"Oh, how *good* of him!" she cried. "I never dreamed they'd be here!"

"Nellie," said I sternly. "You never told me you were married!"

"Why should I?" she asked innocently. "You never asked me."

I had not. I had seen that she signed her name "Ellen Robertson," and I knew she was president of a college - how could I imagine her married. Married she evidently was, and even her long-lost brother was forgotten for a moment as the big man engulfed her in his gray overcoat, and the tall son and daughter added their arms to the group.

But it was only a moment, and the big brotherly grasp of my new relation's hand, the cordial nephewly grip, and affectionate niecely kiss gave me a new and unexpected sense of the joys of homecoming.

These were people, real people, as warm and kind and cheery as people ever were; and they greeted me with evident good will. It was "Uncle John" in no time, and Hallie in especial seized upon me as her own.

"I know mother's got you all broken in by this time," she said. "And that you are prepared for all manner of amazing disclosures. But Mother never told us how handsome you are, Uncle John!"

"In vain is the net spread in sight of any bird," murmured young Jerrold mischievously.

"Don't listen to him, Uncle! I am perfectly sincere," she protested, leaning over to hug her mother again, and turning back to me with a confiding smile.

"Why should I doubt such evident good judgment?" said I. And she slipped her hand in mine and squeezed it. Nellie sat there, looking as proud and happy and matronly and motherly as anybody could, and a great weight rolled off my heart. Some things were left of my old world anyway.

We talked gaily and excitedly on our way of immediate plans, rolling smoothly along broad, open streets. A temporary conclusion was to stop at Hallie's apartment for the time being; and I was conscious of a distinct sense of loss to think of my new-found niece being already married.

"How still it is!" I presently observed. "Is that because it is afternoon, too?"

"Oh, no," they assured me. "We aren't as noisy as we used to be."

"These children don't know anything about what we used to have to put up with," said Owen. "They never were in New York while it was screaming. You see, there are no horses; all surface vehicles are rubber-tired; the minor delivery is pneumatic, and the freight all goes underneath - on those silent monorails."

The great city spread about us, clean as a floor, quiet as a country town by comparison with what I remembered; yet full of the stir and murmur of moving crowds. Everyone we passed or met looked happy and prosperous, and even my inexperienced eye caught a difference in costuming.

"There's no masquerade on, is there?" I asked.

"Oh, no - we all wear what we please, that's all. Don't you like it?" Nellie asked.

Generally there appeared the trim short skirt I had noticed as so appropriate on ship-board; here and there a sort of Florentine gown, long, richly damasked; sometimes a Greekish flow of drapery; the men mostly knickerbockered. I couldn't deny that it was pleasant to the eye, but it worried me a little none the less.

"There's no hurry, John," said Nellie, always unobtrusively watching me. "Some things you'll just have to get used to."

"Before I wholly accept this sudden new brother," I presently suggested, "I'd like to know his name."

"Montrose - Owen Montrose, at your service," he said, bowing his fine head. "Also Jerrold Montrose - and Hallie Robertson!"

"Dear, dear!" I protested. So it's come to that, has it?"

"It's come to that - and we still love each other!" Nellie cheerfully agreed.

"But it isn't final. There's a strong movement on foot to drop hereditary names altogether."

I groaned. "In the name of common humanity, don't tell me anything worse than you have now!"

Hallie's apartment was in a big building, far uptown, overlooking the Hudson

"I have to live in town nine months of the year, you see, Uncle, on account of my work," she explained rather apologetically.

"Hallie's an official - and awfully proud of it," her brother whispered very loudly.

"Jerrold's only a musician - and pretends to be proud of it!" she retorted. Whereat he forcibly held and kissed her.

I could see no very strong difference between this brother and sister and others I had known - except that they were perhaps unusually affectionate.

It was a big, handsome place. The front windows faced the great river, the rear ones opened on a most unexpected scene of loveliness. A big sheltered garden, every wall-space surrounding it a joy to the eye - rich masses of climbing vines, a few trees, a quiet fountain, beautiful stone seats and winding walks, flowers in profusion, and birds singing.

"We used to have only the song of the tomcat in my time. Have you taught the cat to lie down with the canary - or killed him?"

"There are no animals kept in cities any more - except the birds - and they come and go."

"Mostly sparrows, I suppose?"

"No; the sparrow went with the horse," Owen replied. "And the mouse, the fly and the croton bug went with the kitchen."

I turned with a gesture of despair.

"No homes left? "

"I didn't say 'home' - I said 'kitchen.'

Brace up, old man! We still eat - and better food than you ever dreamed of in your hungriest youth."

"That's a long story," Nellie here suggested. "We mustn't crowd him. Let's get washed and rested a bit, and have some of that food you're boasting of."

They gave me a room with a river window, and I looked out at the broad current, changed only in its lovely clearness, and at the changeless Palisades.

Changeless? I started, and seized the traveling glass still on the strap.

The high cliffs reached away to the northward, still wooded, though sprinkled with buildings; but the more broken section opposite the city was a picture of startling beauty.

The water front was green-parked, white-piered, rimmed with palaces, and the broken slopes terraced and garlanded in rich foliage. White cottages and larger buildings climbed and nestled along the sunny slopes as on the cliffs at Capri. It was a place one would go far to see.

I dropped my eyes to the nearer shore.

Again the park, the boulevard, the gracious outlines of fine architecture.

It was beautiful - undeniably beautiful - but a strange world to me. I felt like one at a play. A plain, ordinary American landscape ought not to look like a theatre curtain!

CHAPTER 4

They called me to supper. "Most of us have our heartiest meal in the middle of the day," my sister said.

"The average man, Victim of Copious Instruction," added my brother-in-law, "does his work in the morning; the two hours that he has to, or the four that he usually puts in. Eight to twelve, or nine to one - that is the working day for everybody. Then home, rest, a bath maybe, and then - allow me to help you to some of our Improvements!"

I was hungry, and this simple meal looked and smelled most appetizing. There was in particular a large shining covered dish, which, being opened, gave forth so savory a steam as fairly to make my mouth water. A crisp and toothsome bread was by my plate; a hot drink, which they laughingly refused to name, proved most agreeable; a suave, cool salad followed; fruits, some of which were new to me, and most delicate little cakes, closed the meal.

They would not tell me a thing, only saying "Have some more!" and I did. Not till I had eaten, with continuous delight, three helpings from the large dish did I notice that it stood alone, so to speak.

Nellie followed my eye with her usual prompt intelligence. "Yes," she said, "this is all. But we can send for other things in the twinkling of an eye; what would you like?"

I leaned back in my chair and looked at her reproachfully. "I would like some of that salad - not very much, please! And some of those Burbankian products yonder, and one particular brown little cake - if I can hold it."

Nellie smiled demurely. "Oh!" she mildly remarked, "I thought for the moment that our little supper seemed scant to you."

I glared at her, retorting, "Now I will not utter the grateful praises that were rising to my lips. I will even try to look critical and dissatisfied." And I did, but they all laughed.

"It's no manner of use, Uncle John," cried my pretty niece; "we saw you eat it."

"'It' indeed!" I protested. "What is this undeniably easy-to-take concoction you have stuffed me with?"

"My esteemed new brother," Owen answered, "we have been considering your case in conclave assembled, and we think it is wiser to feed you for awhile and demand by all the rites of hospitality that you eat what is set before you and ask no questions for conscience sake. When you begin to pine, to lose your appetite, to look wan and hollow-eyed, then we may reconsider. Meanwhile we will tell you everything you want to know about food in general, and even some particulars - present dishes always excepted."

"I will now produce information," began Hallie, "my office being that of Food Inspector."

"Her main purpose in bringing you here, Uncle, was to give you food and then talk about it," said Jerrold solemnly. Hallie only made a face at him, and went on:

"We have a magnificent system of production and distribution," she explained, "with a decreasing use of animal foods."

"Was this a vegetarian meal?" I asked in a hollow voice.

"Mostly; but you shall have meat when you want it - better meat than you used to get, too."

"Cold Storage Meat?"

"Oh, no; that's long since stopped. The way we manage about meat is this: A proper proportion of edible animals are raised under good conditions - nice, healthy, happy beasts; killed so that they don't know it! - and never kept beyond a certain time limit.

"You see," she paused, looking for the moment like her mother, "the whole food business is changed - you don't realize."

"Go ahead and tell me - tell me all - my life at present is that of Rollo, I perceive, and I am most complacent after this meal."

"Uncle, I rejoice in your discovery, I do indeed. You are an uncle after my own heart," said Jerrold.

So my fair niece, looking like any other charming girl in a pretty evening frock, began to expound her specialty. Her mother begged to interrupt for the moment. "Let me recall to him things as they were - which you hardly know, you happy child. .Don't forget, John, that when we were young we did not know what good food was."

I started to protest, but she shook her finger at me.

"No, we didn't, my dear boy. We knew 'what we liked,' as the people said at the picture show; but that did not make it good - good in itself or good for us. The world was ill-fed. Most of the food was below par; a good deal was injurious, some absolutely poison. People sold poison for food in 1910, don't forget that! You may remember the row that was beginning to be made about it."

I admitted recalling something of the sort, though it had not particularly interested me at the time.

"Well, that row went on - and gained in force. The women woke up."

"If you have said that once since we met, my dear sister, you've said it forty times. I wish you would make a parenthesis in these food discussions and tell me how, when and why the women woke up."

Nellie looked a little dashed, and Owen laughed outright.

"You stand up for your rights, John!" he said, rising and slapping me on the shoulder. "Let's go in the other room and settle down for a chin - it's our fate."

"Hold him till he sees our housekeeping," said Jerrold. I stood watching, while they rapidly placed our dishes - which I now noticed were very few - in a neat square case which stood on a side table. Everything went in out of sight; paper napkins from the same receptacle wiped the shining table; and then a smooth-running dumbwaiter took it from our sight.

"This is housework," said Nellie, mischievously.

"I refuse to be impressed. Come back to our muttons," I insisted. "You can tell me about your domestic sleight-of-hand in due season."

So we lounged in the large and pleasant parlor, the broad river before us, rimmed with starry lamps, sparkling everywhere with the lights of tiny pleasure craft, and occasionally the blaze and wash of larger boats. I had a sense of pleasant well-being. I had eaten heartily, very heartily, yet was not oppressed. My new-found family pleased me well. The quiet room was beautiful in color and proportion, and as my eyes wandered idly over it I noted how few in number and how harmonious were its contents giving a sense of peace and spaciousness.

The air was sweet - I did not notice then, as I did later, that the whole city was sweet-aired now; at least by comparison with what cities used to be. From somewhere came the sound of soft music, grateful to the ear. I stretched myself luxuriously with:

"Now, then, Nellie - let her go - 'the women woke up.' "

"Some women were waking up tremendously, before you left, John Robertson, only I dare say you never noticed it. They just kept on, faster and faster, till they all did - about all. There are some Dodos left, even yet, but they don't count - discredited grandmothers!"

"And, being awake?" I gently suggested.

"And being awake, they" She paused for an instant, seeking an expression, and Jerrold's smooth bass voice put in, "They saw their duty and they did it."

"Exactly," his mother agreed, with a proudly loving glance at him; "that's just what they did! And in regard to the food business, they recognized at last that it was their duty to feed the world - and that it was miserably done! So they took hold."

"Now, mother, this is my specialty," Hallie interposed.

"When a person can only talk about one thing, why oppose them?" murmured Jerrold. But she quite ignored him, and re - opened her discussion.

"We - that is, most of the women and some of the men - began to seriously study the food question, both from a hygienic and an economic standpoint. I can't tell you that thirty years' work in a minute, Uncle John, but here's the way we manage it now: We have learned very definitely what people ought not to eat, and it is not only a punishable, but a punished offense to sell improper food stuffs."

"How are the people to know?" I ventured.

"The people are not required to know everything. All the food is watched and tested by specialists; what goes into the market is good - all of it."

"By impeccable angelic specialists - like my niece?"

She shook her head at me. "If they were not, the purchaser would spot them at once. You see, our food supply is not at the mercy of the millions of ignorant housewives any more. Food is bought and prepared by people who know how - and they have all the means - and knowledge - for expert tests."

"And if the purchaser too was humanly fallible? "

She cast a pitying glance on me, and her father took the floor for a moment.

"You see, John, in the old time the dealers were mostly poor, and sold cheap and bad stuff to make a little money. The buyers were mostly poor, and had to buy the cheap and nasty stuff. Even large manufacturers were under pressure, and had to cheat to make a profit - or thought they had to. Then when we got to inspectors and such like they were under the harrow, too, and were by no means impeccable. Our big change is this: Nobody is poor now."

"I hear you say that," I answered, "but I can't seem to get it through my head. Have you really divided all the property?"

"John Robertson, I'm ashamed of you!" cried Nellie. "Even in 1910 people knew better than that - people who knew anything!"

"That wasn't necessary," said Owen, "nor desirable. What we have done is this: First, we have raised the productive capacity of the population; second, we have secured their right to our natural resources; third, we have learned to administer business without waste. The wealth of the world grows enormously. It is not what you call 'equally distributed,' but every one has enough. There is no economic danger any more; there is economic peace."

"And economic freedom?" asked I sharply.

"And economic freedom. People choose the work they like best, and work - freely, more than they have to."

I pondered on this. "Ah, but they *have to* - labor is compulsory."

Owen grinned. "Yes, labor is compulsory - always was. It is compulsory on everyone now. We used to have two sets who wouldn't work - paupers and the idle rich; no such classes left - all busy."

"But, the freedom of the individual " I persisted.

"Come, come, brother; society always played hob with the freedom of the individuals whenever it saw fit. It killed, imprisoned, fined; it had compulsory laws and regulations; it required people to wear clothes and furnished no clothes for them to wear. If society has a right to take human life, why has it not a right to improve it? No, my dear man," continued Owen (he was evidently launched on *his* specialty now) "society is not somebody else domineering over us! Society is us - taking care of ourselves."

I took no exception to this, and he began again. "Society, in our young days, was in a state of auto-intoxication. It generated its own poisons, and absorbed them in peaceful, slow suicide. To think! - it seems im possible now - to *think* of allowing anybody to sell bad food!"

"That wasn't the only bad thing they sold" I suggested.

"No; unfortunately. Why, look here - " Owen slid a glass panel in the wall and took out a book.

"That's clever," I remarked approvingly, "Bookcases built in!"

"Yes, they are everywhere now," said Nellie. Books - a few of them - are common human necessities. Every home, every room almost, has these little dust-tight, insect-proof wall cases. Concrete construction has helped very much in all such matters."

Owen had found his place, and now poured upon me a concentrated list of the adulterated materials deteriorating the world in that period so slightingly referred to as "my day." I noticed with gratitude that Owen said "When we were young!"

"You never were sure of getting *anything* pure," he said scornfully, "no matter what you paid for it. How we submitted to such rank outrage for so long I cannot imagine! This was taken up very definitely some twenty years ago, by the women mostly."

"Aha - 'when the women woke up!' " I cried.

"Yes, just that. It is true that their being mostly mere housewives and seamstresses was a handicap in some ways; but it was a direct advantage in others. They were almost all consumers, you see, not producers. They were not so much influenced by considerations of the profits of the manufacturer as they were by the direct loss to their own pockets and health. Yes," he smiled reminiscently, "there were some pretty warm years while this thing was thrashed out. One of the most successful lines of attack was in the New Food system, though."

"I *will* talk!" cried Hallie. "Here I've inveigled Uncle John up here - and - and fed him to repletion; and have him completely at my mercy, and then you people butt in and do all the talking!"

"Go it, little sister - you're dead right!" agreed Jerrold, "You see, Uncle, it's one thing to restrain and prevent and punish - and another thing to substitute improvements."

"Kindergarten methods?" I ventured.

"Yes, exactly. As women had learned this in handling children, they began to apply it to grown people - the same children, only a little older. Ever so many people had been talking and writing about this food business, and finally some of them got together and really started it."

"One of these cooperative schemes?" I was beginning, but the women looked at me with such pitying contempt that I promptly withdrew the suggestion.

"Not much!" said Nellie disdainfully. "Of course, those cooperative schemes were a natural result of the growing difficulties in our old methods, but they were on utterly wrong lines. No, sir; the new food business was a real business, and a very successful one. The first company began about 1912 or '13, I think. Just some women with a real business sense, and enough capital. They wisely concluded that a block of apartments was the natural field for their services; and that professional women were their natural patrons."

"The unprofessional women - or professional wives, as you might call them - had only their housewifery to preserve their self-respect, you see," put in Owen. "If they didn't do housekeeping for a living, what - in the name of decency - did they do?"

"This was called the Home Service Company," said Hallie. "(I will talk, mother!) They built some unusually attractive apartments, planned by women, to please women; this block was one of the finest designs of their architects - women, too, by the way."

"Who had waked up," murmured Jerrold, unnoticed.

"It was frankly advertised as specially designed for professional women. They looked at it, liked it, and moved in; teachers, largely doctors, lawyers, dressmakers; women who worked."

Sort of a nunnery?" I asked.

"My dear brother, do you imagine that all working women were orphan spinsters, even in your day?" cried Nellie. "The self-supporting women of that time generally had other people to support, too. Lots of them were married; many were widows with children; even the single ones had brothers and sisters to take care of."

"They rushed in, anyhow," said Hallie. "The place was beautiful and built for enjoyment. There was a nice garden in the middle "

"Like this one here?" I interrupted. "This is a charming patio. How did they make space for it?"

"New York blocks were not divinely ordained," Owen replied. "It occurred to the citizens at last they they could bisect those 200 x 800-foot oblongs, and they did. Wide, tree-shaded, pleasant ways run between the old avenues, and the blocks remaining are practically squares."

"You noticed the irregular border of grass and shrubbery as we came up, didn't you, Uncle?" asked Jerrold. "We forgot to speak about it, because we are used to it."

I did recall now that our ride had been not through monotonous, stone-faced, right-angled ravines, but along the pleasant fronts of gracious varying buildings, whose skyline was a pleasure and street line bordered greenly,

"You didn't live here and don't remember, maybe," Owen remarked, "but the regular thing uptown was one of those lean, long blocks, flat-faced and solid, built to the side-walk's edge. If it was a line of private houses they were bordered with gloomy little stone-paved areas, and ornamented with ash-cans and garbage pails. If the avenue end was faced with tall apartments, their lower margin was infested with a row of little shops - meat, fish, vegetable, fruit - with all their litter and refuse and flies, and constant traffic. Now a residence block is a thing of beauty on all sides. The really necessary shops are maintained, but planned for in the building, and made beautiful. Those fly-tainted meat markets no longer exist."

"I *will* talk!" said Hallie, so plaintively that we all laughed and let her.

"That first one I was telling you about was very charming and attractive. There were arrangements on the top floor for nurseries and child gardens; and the roof was for children all day; evenings the grown-ups had it. Great care was taken by the management in letting this part to the best professionals in child culture.

"There were big rooms, too, for meetings and parties; places for billiards and bowling and swimming - it was planned for real human enjoyment, like a summer hotel."

"But I thought you said this place was for women," I incautiously ventured.

"Oh, Uncle John! And has it never occurred to you that women like to amuse themselves? Or that professional women have men relatives and men friends? There were plenty of men in the building, and plenty more to visit it. They were shown how nice it was, you see. But the chief card was the food and service. This company engaged, at high wages, first-class houseworkers, and the residents paid for them by the hour; and they had a food service which was beyond the dreams of - of - homes, or boarding houses."

"Your professional women must have been millionaires," I mildly suggested.

"You think so because you do not understand the food business, Uncle John; nobody did in those days. We were so used to the criminal waste of individual house-keeping, with its pitifully low standards, and to monotonous low-grade restaurant meals, with their waste and extortion, that it never occurred to us to estimate the amount of profit there really was in the business. These far-seeing women were pioneers - but not for long! Dozens are claiming first place now, just as the early 'Women's Clubs' used to.

"They established in that block a meal service that was a wonder for excellence, and for cheapness, too; and people began to learn."

I was impressed, but not convinced, and she saw it.

"Look here, Uncle John, I hate to use figures on a helpless listener, but you drive me to it."

Then she reached for the bookcase and produced her evidence, sparingly, but with effect. She showed me that the difference between the expense of hiring separate service and the same number of people patronizing a service company was sufficient to reduce expenses to the patrons and leave a handsome payment for the company

Owen looked on, interpreting to my ignorance.

"You never kept house, old, man," he said, "nor thought much about it, I expect; but you can figure this out for yourself easily enough. Here were a hundred families, equal to, say, five hundred persons. They hired a hundred cooks, of course; paid them something like six dollars a week - call it five on an average. There's $500 a week, just for cooks - $26,000 a year!

"Now, as a matter of fact (our learned daughter tells us this), ten cooks are plenty for five hundred persons - at the same price would cost $1,300 a year!"

"Ten are plenty, and to spare," said Hallie; "but we pay them handsomely. One chef at $3,000; two next bests at $2,000 each, four thousand; two at $1,000 apiece, two thousand; five at $800, four thousand. That's $18,000 - half what we paid before, and the difference in service between a kitchen maid and a scientific artist."

"Fifty per cent, saved on wages, and 500 per cent, added to skill," Owen continued. "And you can go right on and add 90 per cent, saving in fuel, 90 per cent, in plant, 50 per cent, in utensils, and - how much is it, Hallie, in materials?"

Hallie looked very important.

"Even when they first started, when food was shamefully expensive and required all manner of tests and examinations, the saving was all of 60 per cent. Now it is fully 80 per cent."

"That makes a good deal all told, Uncle John," Jerrold quietly remarked, handing me a bit of paper. "You see, it does leave a margin of profit."

I looked rather helplessly at the figures; also at Hallie.

"It is a shame, Uncle, to hurry you so, but the sooner you get these little matters clear in your head, the better. We have these great food furnishing companies, now, all over the country; and they have market gardens and dairies and so on, of their own. There is a Food Bureau in every city, and a National Food Bureau, with international relations. The best scientific knowledge is used to study food values, to improve old materials and develop new ones; there's a tremendous gain."

"But - do the people swallow things as directed by the government?" I protested. "Is there no chance to go and buy what you want to eat when you want it?"

They rose to their feet with one accord. Jerrold seized me by the hand.

"Come on, Uncle!" he cried. "Now is as good a time as any. You shall see our food department - come to scoff and remain to prey - if you like."

The elevator took us down, and I was led unresistingly among their shining modernities.

"Here is the source of supply," said Owen, showing where the basement supply room connected with a clean, airy subway under the glass-paved sidewalk. "Ice we make, drinking water we distil, fuel is wired to us; but the food stuffs are brought this way. Come down early enough and you would find these arteries of the city flowing steadily with "

"Milk and honey," put in Jerrold.

"With the milk train, the meat train, the vegetable train, and so on."

"Ordered beforehand?" I asked.

"Ordered beforehand. Up to midnight you may send down word as to the kind of mushrooms you prefer - and no extra charge. During the day you can still order, but there's a trifle more expense - not much. But most of us are more than content to have our managers cater for us. From the home outfit you may choose at any time. There are lists upstairs, and here is the array."

There were but few officials in this part of the great establishment at this hour, but we were politely shown about by a scholarly looking man in white linen, who had been reading as we entered. They took me between rows of glass cases, standing as books do in the library, and showed me the day's baking; the year's preserves; the fragrant, colorful shelves of such fruit and vegetables as were not fresh picked from day to day.

"We don't get today's strawberries till the local ones are ripe," Jerrold told us. "These are yesterday's, and pretty good yet."

"Excuse me, but those have just come in," said the white-linen person; "this morning's picking, from Maryland."

I tasted them with warm approval. There was a fascinating display of cakes and cookies, some old favorites, some of a new but attractive aspect; and in glass-doored separate ice-chambers, meats, fish, milk, and butter.

"Can people come in here and get what they want, though?" I inquired triumphantly.

"They can, and occasionally they do. But what it will take you some time to realize, John," my sister explained, "is the different attitude of people toward their food. We are all not only well fed - sufficiently fed - but so wisely fed that we seldom think of wanting anything further. When we do we can order from upstairs, come down to the eating room and order, send to the big depots if it is some rare thing, or even come in like this. To the regular purchasers it is practically free,"

"And how if you are a stranger - a man in the street?"

"In every city in our land you may go into any eating house and find food as good - and cheap - as this," said Hallie, triumphantly.

CHAPTER 5

While below they took me into the patio, that quiet inner garden which was so attractive from above. It was a lovely place. The moon was riding high and shone down into it; a slender fountain spray rose shimmering from its carved basin; on the southern-facing wall a great wistaria vine drooped in budding purple, and beds of violets made the air rich with soft fragrance.

Here and there were people walking; and in the shadowy corners sat young couples, apparently quite happy.

"I suppose you don't know the names of one of them," I suggested.

"On the contrary, I know nearly all," answered Hallie. "These apartments are taken very largely by friends and acquaintances. You see, the gardens and roofs are in common, and there are the reading-rooms, ballrooms, and so on. It is pleasanter to be friends to begin with, and most of us get to be afterward, if we are not at first.

"But surely there are some disagreeable people left on earth!"

"Yes; but where there is so much more social life people get together in congenial sets," put in Nellie; "just as we used to in summer resorts.,,

"There aren't so many bores and fools as there used to be, John," Owen remarked. "We really do raise better people. Even the old ones have improved. You see, life is so much pleasanter and more interesting."

"We're all healthier, Uncle John, because we're better fed; that makes us more agreeable."

"There's more art in the world to make us happier," said Jerrold. Hallie thinks it's all due to her everlasting bread and butter. Listen to that now!"

From a balcony up there in the moonlight came a delicious burst of melody; a guitar and two voices, and the refrain was taken up from another window, from one corner of the garden, from the roof; all in smooth accord.

"Your group here must be an operatic one," I suggested. But my nephew answered that it was not, but that music - good music - was so common now, and so well taught, that the average was high in both taste and execution.

We sat late that night, my new family bubbling over with things to say, and filling my mind with a confused sense of new advantages, unexplained and only half believed.

I could not bring myself to accept as commonplace facts the unusual excellences so glibly described, and I suppose my silence showed this as well as what I said, for my sister presently intervened with decision:

"We must all stop this for tonight," she said. "John feels as if he was being forcibly fed - he's got to rest. Then I suggest that tomorrow Owen take him in hand - go off for a tramp, why don't you? - and really straighten out things. You see, there are two distinct movements to consider, the unconscious progress that would have taken place anyway in thirty years, and then the deliberate measures adopted by the 'New Lifers,' and it's rather confusing. I've labored with him all the way home now; I think the man's point of view will help."

Owen was a big man with a strong, wholesome face, and a quizzical little smile of his own. He and I went up the river next morning in a swift motor boat, which did not batter the still air with muffled banging as they used to do, and strolled off in the bright spring sunshine into Palisade Park.

"We've saved all the loveliest of it - for keeps," he said. "Out here, where the grass and trees are just as they used to be, you won't be bothered, and one expositor will be easier to handle than four at once. Now, shall I talk, or will you ask questions?"

"I'd like to ask a few questions first, then you can expound by the hour. Do give me the long and short of this 'Women-waked-up' proposition. What does it mean - to a man?"

Owen stroked his chin.

"No loss," he said at length; "at least, no loss that's not covered by a greater gain. Do you remember the new biological theory in regard to the relative position of the sexes that was beginning to make headway when we were young?"

I nodded. "Ward's theory? Oh, yes; I heard something of it. Pretty far-fetched, it seemed to me."

"Far-fetched and dear-bought, but true for all that. You'll have to swallow it. The female is the race type; the male is her assistant. It's established beyond peradventure."

I meditated, painfully. I looked at Owen. He had just as happy and proud a look as if he was a real man - not merely an Assistant. I though of Jerrold - nothing cowed about him; of the officers and men on the ship; of such men as I had seen in the street.

"I suppose this applies in the main to remote origins?" I suggested.

"It holds good all through life - is just as true as it ever was."

"Then - do you mean that women run everything, and men are only helpers?"

"Oh, no; I wasn't talking about human life at all - only about sex. 'Running things' has nothing to do with that. Women run some businesses and are in practically all, but men still do the bulk of the world's work. There is a natural division of labor, after all."

This was pleasant to hear, but he dashed my hopes.

"Men do almost all the violent plain work - digging and hewing and hammering; women, as a class, prefer the administrative and constructive kinds. But all that is open yet, and settling itself gradually; men and women are working everywhere. The big change which Nellie is always referring to means simply that women 'waked up' to a realization of the fact that they were human beings."

"What were they before, pray?"

"Only female beings."

"Female human beings, of course," said I.

"Yes; a little human, but mostly female. Now they are mostly human. It is a great change."

"I don't follow you. Aren't they still wives and mothers?"

"They are still mothers - far more so than they were before, as a matter of fact; but as to being wives - there's a difference."

I was displeased, and showed it.

"Well, is it Polygamy, or Polyandry, or Trial Marriages, or what?"

Owen gazed at me with an expression very like Nellie's.

"There it is," he said. "You can only think about women in some sort of relation to men, of a change in marriage relations as merely a change in kind; whereas what has happened is a change in *degree*. We still have monogamous marriages, on a much purer and more lasting plane than a generation ago; but the word 'wife' does not mean what it used to."

"Go on - I can't follow you at all."

"A 'wife' used to be a possession; 'wilt thou be mine?' said the lover, and the wife was his."

"Well - whose else is she now?" I asked with some sharpness.

"She does not 'belong' to anyone in that old sense. She is the wife of her husband in that she is his true lover, and that their marriage is legally recorded; but her life and work does not belong to him. He has no right to her 'services' any more. A woman who is in a business - like Hallie, for instance - does not give it up when she marries."

I stopped him. "What! Isn't Hallie married?"

"No - not yet."

"But - that is her flat?"

Yes; why not?" He laughed at me. "You see, you can't imagine a woman having a home of her own. Hallie is twenty-three. She won't marry for some years, probably; but she has her position and is doing excellent work. It's only a minor inspectorship, but she likes it. Why shouldn't she have a home?"

"Why doesn't she have it with you?"

"Because I like to live with my wife. Her business, and mine, are in Michigan; Hallie's in New York."

"And when she marries she keeps on being an inspector?" I queried.

"Precisely. The man who marries that young woman will have much happiness, but he will not 'own' her, and she will not be his wife in the sense of a servant. She will not darn his socks or cook his meals. Why should she?"

"Will she not nurse his babies?"

"No; she will nurse *her* babies - *their* babies, not 'his' merely."

"And keep on being an inspector?"

"And keep on being an inspector - for four hours a day - in two shifts. Not a bit more difficult than cooking, my dear boy."

"But - she will not be with her children - "

"She will be with her children twenty hours out of the twenty-four - if she wants to. But Hallie's not specially good with children. . . . You see, John, the women have specialized - even in motherhood." Then he went on at considerable length to show how there had arisen a recognition of far more efficient motherhood than was being given; that those women best fitted for the work had given eager, devoted lives to it and built up a new science of Humaniculture; that no woman was allowed to care for her children without proof of capacity.

"Allowed by whom?" I put in.

"By the other women - the Department of Child Culture - the Government."

"And the fathers - do they submit to this, tamely?"

"No; they cheerfully agree and approve. Absolutely the biggest thing that has happened, some of us think, is that new recognition of the importance of childhood. We are raising better people now."

I was silent for a while, pulling up bits of grass and snapping small sticks into inch pieces.

"There was a good deal of talk about Eugenics, I remember," I said at last, "and - what was that thing? Endowment of Motherhood?"

"Yes - man's talk," Owen explained. "You see, John, we couldn't look at women but in one way - in the old days; it was all a question of sex with us - inevitably, we being males. Our whole idea of improvement was in better breeding; our whole idea of motherhood was in each woman's devoting her whole life to her own children. That turbid freshet of an Englishman, Wells, who did so much to stir his generation, said 'I am wholly feminist' - and he was! He saw women only as females and wanted them endowed as such. He was never able to see them as human beings and amply competent to take care of themselves.

"Now, our women, getting hold of this idea that they really are human creatures, simply blossomed forth in new efficiency. They specialized the food business - Hallie's right about the importance of that - and then they specialized the baby business. All women who wish to, have babies; but if they wish to take care of them they must show a diploma."

I looked at him. I didn't like it - but what difference did that make? I had died thirty years ago, it appeared.

"A diploma for motherhood!" I repeated; but he corrected me.

"Not at all. Any woman can be a mother - if she's normal. I said she had to have a diploma as a child-culturist - quite a different matter."

"I don't see the difference."

"No, I suppose not. I didn't, once," he said. "Any and every mother was supposed to be competent to 'raise' children - and look at the kind of people we raised! You see, we are beginning to learn - just beginning. You needn't imagine that we are in a state of perfection - there are more new projects up for discussion than ever before. We've only made a start. The consequences, so far, are so good that we are boiling over with propositions for future steps."

"Go on about the women," I said. "I want to know the worst and become resigned."

"There's nothing very bad to tell," he continued cheerfully. "When a girl is born she is treated in all ways as if she was a boy; there is no hint made in any distinction between them except in the perfectly open physiological instruction as to their future duties. Children, young humans, grow up under precisely the same conditions. I speak, of course, of the most advanced people - there are still backward places - there's plenty to do yet.

"Then the growing girls are taught of their place and power as mothers - and they have tremendously high ideals. That's what has done so much to raise the standard in men. It came hard, but it worked."

I raised my head with keen interest, remarking, "I've glimpsed a sort of Iron hand in a velvet glove back of all this. What did they do?"

Owen looked rather grim for a moment.

"The worst of it was twenty or twenty-five years back. Most of those men are dead. That new religious movement stirred the socio-ethical sense to sudden power; it coincided with the women's political movement, urging measures for social improvement; its enormous spread, both by preaching and literature, lit up the whole community with new facts, ideas and feelings. Health - physical purity - was made a practical ideal. The young women learned the proportion of men with syphilis and gonorrhoea and decided it was wrong to marry them. That was enough. They passed laws in every State requiring a clean bill of health with every marriage license. Diseased men had to die bachelors - that's all."

"And did men submit to legislation like that?" I protested.

"Why not? It was so patently for the protection of the race - of the family - of the women and children. Women were solid for it, of course - And all the best men with them. To oppose it was almost a confession of guilt and injured a man's chances of marriage."

"It used to be said that any man could find a woman to marry him," I murmured, meditatively.

"Maybe he could - once. He certainly cannot now. A man who has one of those diseases is so reported - just like small-pox, you see. Moreover, it is registered against him by the Department of Eugenics - physicians are required to send in lists; any girl can find out."

"It must have left a large proportion of unmarried women."

"It did, at first. And that very thing was of great value to the world. They were wise, conscientious, strong women, you see, and they poured all their tremendous force into social service. Lots of them went into child culture - used their mother-power that way. It wasn't easy for them; it wasn't easy for the left-over men, either!"

"It must have increased prostitution to an awful extent," I said.

Owen shook his head and regarded me quizzically.

"That is the worst of it," he said. "There isn't any."

I sat up. I stood up. I walked up and down. "No prostitution! I— I can't believe it. Why, prostitution is a social necessity, as old as Nineveh!".

Owen laughed outright. "Too late, old man; too late! I know we used to think so. We did use to call it a 'social necessity,' didn't we? Come, now, tell me what necessity it was *to the women.*"

I stopped my march and looked at him.

"To the women," he repeated. "What did they want of prostitution? What good did it do them?"

"Why - why - they made a living at it," I replied, rather lamely.

"Yes, a nice, honorable, pleasant, healthy living, didn't they? With all women perfectly well able to earn an excellent living decently; with all women fully educated about these matters and knowing what a horrible death was before them in this business; with all women brought up like human beings and not like over-sexed female animals, and with all women quite free to marry if they wished to - how many, do you think, would choose that kind of business?

"We never waited for them to choose it, remember! We fooled them and lied to them and dragged them in - and drove them in - forced them in - and kept them as slaves and prisoners. They didn't really enjoy the life; you know that. Why should they go into it if they do not have to - to accommodate us?"

"Do you mean to tell me there are no - wantons - among women?" I demanded.

"No, I don't mean any such thing. There are various kinds of over-developed and morbidly developed women as there are men, and we haven't weeded them out entirely. But the whole thing is now recognized as pathological - cases for medical treatment, or perhaps surgical. Besides, wantonness is not prostitution. Prostitution is a social crime of the worst order. No one thing did more harm. The women stamped it out."

"Legislated us all into morality, did they?" I inquired sarcastically.

"Legislation did a good deal; education did more; the new religion did most; social opinion helped. You remember we men never really tried to legislate against prostitution - we wanted it to go on."

"Why, surely we did legislate against it - and it was of no use!" I protested.

"No; we legislated against the women, but not against the men, or the thing itself. We examined the women, and fined them, and licensed them - and never did anything against the men. Women legislators used very different measures, I assure you."

"I suppose it is for the good of the world," I presently admitted; "but... "

"But you don't quite like to think of men in this new and peculiar position of having to be good!"

"Frankly - I don't. I'm willing to be good, but - I don't like to be given no choice."

"Well, now, look at it. As it was, we had one way, according to what we thought was good for us. Rather than lead clean, contented lives at some expense to ourselves in the way of moral and physical control, we deliberately sacrificed an army of women to a horrible life and a more horrible death, and corrupted the blood of the nation. It was on the line of health they made their stand, not on 'morality' alone. Under our new laws it is held a crime to poison another human being with syphilis, just as much as to use prussic acid."

"Nellie said you had no crime now."

"Oh, well, Nellie is an optimist. I suppose she meant the old kinds and definitions. We don't call things 'crimes' any more. And then, really, there is not a hundredth part of the evil done that there used to be. We know more, you see, and have less temptation."

We were silent for a while. I watched a gull float and wheel over the blue water. Big airships flew steadily along certain lines. Little ones sailed about on all sides.

One darted over our heads and lit with a soft swoop on an open promontory.

"Didn't they use to buzz?" I asked Owen.

"Of course; just as the first motor boats thumped and banged abominably. We will not stand for unnecessary noise, as we used to."

"How do you stop it? More interference with the individual rights?"

"More recognition of public rights. A bad noise is a nuisance, like a bad smell. We didn't used to mind it much - but the women did. You see, what women like has to be considered now."

"It always was considered!" I broke in with some heat. "The women of America were the most spoiled, pampered lot on earth; men gave up to them in all ways."

"At home, perhaps, but not in public. The city and state weren't run to suit them at all."

"Why should they be? Women belong at home. If they push into a man's world they ought to take the consequences."

Owen stretched his long legs and looked up at the soft, brilliant blue above us.

"Why do you call the world "man's?" he asked.

"It *was* man's; it ought to be. Woman's place is in the home. I suppose I sound like ancient history to you?" and I laughed a little shamefacedly.

"We *have* rather lost that point of view," Owen guardedly admitted. "You see" and then he laughed. "It's no use, John; no matter how we put it to you it's a jar. The world's thought has changed - and you have got to catch up!"

"Suppose I refuse? Suppose I really am unable?"

"We won't suppose it for a moment," he said cheerfully. "Ideas are not nailed down. Just take out what you had and insert some new ones. Women are people - just as much as we are; that's a *fact*, my dear fellow. You'll have to accept it."

"And are men allowed to be people, too?" I asked gloomily.

"Why, of course! Nothing has interfered with our position as human beings; it is only our sex supremacy that we have lost."

"And do you *like* it?" I demanded.

"Some men made a good deal of fuss at first - the old-fashioned kind, and all the worst varieties. But modern men aren't worried in the least over their position. . .

See here, John, you don't grasp this - women are vastly more agreeable than they used to be."

I looked at him in amazement.

"Fact!" he said. "Of course, we loved our own mothers and daughters and sisters, more or less, no matter how they looked or what they did; and when we were 'in love' there was no limit to the glory of 'the beloved object.' But you and I know that women were pretty unsatisfactory in the old days."

I refused to admit it, but he went on calmly.

"The 'wife and mother' was generally a tired, nervous, overworked creature. She soon lost her beauty and vigor, her charm and inspiration. We were forever chasing fine, handsome, highly desirable young girls, and forever reducing them to weary, worn-out women - in the name of love! The gay outsiders were always a fresh attraction - as long as we couldn't have them. . . . See here, John, can't you understand? Our old way of using women wasn't good for them - nor for us, either, by the way - but it simply spoiled the women. They were hopelessly out of the running with us in all human lines; their business was housework, and ours was world work. There was very little real companionship.

"Now women are intelligent, experienced, well-trained citizens, fully our equals in any line of work they take up, and with us everywhere. It's made the world over!"

"Made it 'feminist' through and through, I suppose!" I groaned.

"Not a bit! It used to be 'masculist' through and through; now it's just *human*. And, see here - women are more attractive, as women, than they used to be."

I stared at this, unbelieving.

"That's true! You see, they are healthy; there's a new standard of physical beauty - very Greek - you must have noticed already the big, vigorous, fresh-colored, free-stepping girls."

I had, even in my brief hours of observation.

"They are far more perfect physically, better developed mentally, with a higher moral sense - yes, you needn't look like that! We used to call them our 'moral superiors,' just because they had the one virtue we insisted on - and we never noticed the lack in other lines. Women today are truthful, brave, honest, generous, self-controlled; they are - jollier, more reasonable, more companionable."

"Well, I'm glad to hear that," I rather grudgingly admitted. "I was afraid they would have lost all - charm."

"Yes, we used to feel that way, I remember. Funny! We were convinced on the one hand that there was nothing to a woman but her eternal womanliness, and on the other we were desperately afraid her womanliness would disappear the moment she turned her mind to anything else. I assure you that men love women, in general and in particular, much more than they used to."

I pondered. "But - what sort of home life do you have?"

"Think for a moment of what we used to have - even in a 'happy home.' The man had the whole responsibility of keeping it up - his business life and interests all foreign to her. She had the whole labor of running it - the direct manual labor in the great majority of cases - the management in any case. They were strangers in an industrial sense.

"When he came home he had to drop all his line of thought - and she hers, except that she generally unloaded on him the burden of inadequacy in housekeeping. Sometimes he unloaded, too. They could sympathize and condole, but neither could help the other.

"The whole thing cost like sin, too. It was a living nightmare to lots of men - and women! The only things they had in common were their children and 'social interests.'

"Well - nowadays, in the first place every body is easy about money. (I'll go into that later.) No woman marries except for love - and good judgment, too; all women are more desirable - more men want to marry them - and that improves the men! You see, a man naturally cares more for women than for anything else in life - and they know it! It's the handle they lift by. That's what has eliminated tobacco."

"Do you mean to say that these women have arbitrarily prevented smoking?" I do not smoke myself, but I was angry nevertheless.

"Not a bit of it, John - not a bit of it. Anybody can smoke who wants to."

"Then why don't they?"

"Because women do not like it."

"What has that to do with it? Can't a man do what he wants to - even if they don't like it?"

"Yes, he can; but it costs too much. Men like tobacco, but they like love better, old man."

"Is it one of your legal requirements for marriage?"

"No, not legal; but women disapprove of tobacco-y lovers, husbands, fathers; they know that the excessive use of it is injurious, and won't marry a heavy smoker. But the main point is that they simply don't like the smell of the stuff, or of the man who uses it - most women, that is."

"But what *difference* does it make? I dare say that most women did not like it before, but surely a man has a right "

"To make himself a disgusting object to his wife," Owen interrupted. "Yes, he has a 'right' to. We would have a right to bang on a tin pan, I suppose - or to burn rubber, but he wouldn't be popular!"

"It's tyranny!" I protested.

"Not at all," he said, imperturbably. "We had no idea what a nuisance we used to be, that's all; or how much women put up with that they did not like at all. I asked a woman once - when I was a bachelor - why she objected to tobacco, and she frankly replied that a man who did not smoke was much pleasanter to kiss! She was a very fascinating little widow - I confess it made me think."

"It's the same with liquor, I suppose? Let's get it all told."

"Yes, only more so. Alcoholism was a race evil of the worst sort. I cannot imagine how we put up with it so long."

"Is this spotless world of yours one solid temperance union?"

"Practically. We use some light wines and a little spirits yet, but infrequently - in this country, at least, and Europe is vastly improved.

"But that was a much more serious thing than the other. It wasn't a mere matter of not marrying! They used all kinds of means. But come on - we'll be late to dinner; and dinner, at least, is still a joy, Brother John."

CHAPTER 6

Out of the mass of information offered by my new family and the pleasant friends we met, together with the books and publications profusely piling around me, I felt it necessary to make a species of digest for my own consideration. This I submitted to Nellie, Owen, and one or two others, adding suggestions and corrections; and thus established in my own mind a coherent view of what had happened.

In the first place, as Owen repeatedly assured me, nothing was *done* - finished - brought to static perfection.

"Thirty years isn't much, you see," he said cheerfully. "I dare say if you'd been here all along you wouldn't think it was such a great advance. We have removed some obvious and utterly unnecessary evils, and cleared the ground for new beginnings; but what we are going to do is the exciting thing!

"Now you think it is so wonderful that we have no poverty. We think it is still more wonderful that a world of even partially sane people could have borne poverty so long."

We naturally discussed this point a good deal, and they brought up a little party of the new economists to enlighten me - Dr. Harkness, sociologist; Mr. Alfred Brown, Department of Production; Mrs. Allerton of the Local Transportation Bureau; and a young fellow named Pike, who had written a little book on "Distinctive Changes of Three Decades," which I found very useful.

"It was such a simple matter, after all, you see," the sociologist explained to me, in an amiable class-room manner.

"Suppose now you were considering the poverty of one family, an isolated family, sir. Now, if this family was poor, it would be due to the limitations of the individual or of the environment. Limitations of the individual would cover inefficiency, false theory of industry, ill-judged division of labor, poor system of production, or misuse of product. Limitation of environment would, of course, apply to climate, soil, natural products, etc. No amount of health, intelligence or virtue could make Iceland rich - if it was completely isolated; nor England, for that matter, owing to the inexorable limitations of that environment.

"Here in this country we have no complaint to make of our natural resources. The soil is capable of sustaining an enormous population. So we have merely to consider the limitations of individuals, transferring our problem from the isolated family to the general public.

"What do we find? All the limitations I enumerated! Inefficiency - nearly every one below par in working power in the generation before last, as well as miserably educated; false theories of industry everywhere - idiotic notions as to what work was 'respectable' and what wasn't, more idiotic notions of payment; worst of all, most idiotic ideas that work was a curse . . . Might as well call digestion a curse! Dear! Dear! How benighted we were!

"Then there was ill-judged division of labor - almost universal; that evil. For instance, look at this one point; half the workers of the world, nearly, were restricted to one class of labor, and that in the lowest industrial grade."

"He means women, in housework, John," Nellie interpolated. "We never used to think of that as part of our economic problem."

"It was a very serious part," the professor continued, hastily forestalling the evident intention of Mr. Brown to strike in, "but there were many others. The obvious utility of natural specialization in labor seemed scarcely to occur to us. Our system of production was archaic in the extreme; practically *no* system was followed."

"You must give credit to the work of the Department of Agriculture, Dr. Harkness," urged Mr. Brown, "the introduction of new fruits, the improvement of stocks "

"Yes, yes," agreed Dr. Harkness, "the rudiments were there, of course; but no real grasp of organized productivity. And as to misuse of product - why, my dear Mr. Robertson, it is a wonder anybody had enough to live on in those days, in view of our criminal waste.

"The real turning point, Mr. Robertson, if we can put our finger on one, is where the majority of the people recognized the folly and evil of poverty - and saw it to be a thing of our own making. We saw that our worst poverty was poverty in the stock - that we raised a terrible percentage of poor people. Then we established a temporary Commission on Human Efficiency, away back in 1913 or 14 "

"Thirteen," put in Mr. Pike, who sat back listening to Dr. Harkness with an air of repressed superiority.

"Thank you," said the eminent sociologist courteously. "These young fellows have it all at their fingers' ends, Mr. Robertson. Better methods in education nowadays, far better! As I was saying, we established a Commission on Human Efficiency."

"You will remember the dawning notions of 'scientific management' we began to have in the first decade of the new century," Mrs. Allerton quietly suggested. "It occurred to us later to apply it to ourselves - and we did."

"The Commission found that the majority of human beings were not properly reared," Dr. Harkness resumed, "with a resultant low standard of efficiency - shockingly low; and that the loss was not merely to the individual but to the community. Then Society stretched out a long arm and took charge of the work of humaniculture - began to lift the human standard.

"I won't burden you with details on that line at present; it touched but one cause of poverty after all. The false theory of industry was next to be changed. A few far-seeing persons were already writing and talking about work as an organic social function, but the sudden spread of it came through the new religion."

"*And* the new voters, Dr. Harkness," my sister added.

He smiled at her benevolently. A large, comfortable, full-bearded, rosy old gentleman was Dr. Harkness, and evidently in full enjoyment of his present task.

"Let us never forget the new voters, of course. They have ceased to be thought of as new, Mr. Robertson - so easily does the human mind accept established conditions. The new religion urged work - normal, well-adapted work - as *the* duty of life - as life itself; and the new voters accepted this idea as one woman.

"They were, as a class, used to doing their duty in patient industry, generally distasteful to them; and the opportunity of doing work they liked - with a sense of higher duty added - was universally welcomed."

"I certainly remember a large class of women who practiced no industry at all - no duty, either, unless what they called 'social duties." I rather sourly remarked. Mrs. Allerton took me up with sudden heat:

"Yes, there were such, in large numbers, in our great cities particularly; but public opinion was rising against them even as far back as 1910. The more progressive women turned the light on them first, and then men took it up and began to see that this domestic pet was not only expensive and useless but injurious and absurd. I don't suppose we can realize," she continued meditatively,

"how complete the change in public opinion is - and how supremely important. In visible material progress we have only followed simple lines, quite natural and obvious, and accomplished what was perfectly possible at any time - if we had only thought so."

"*That's* the point!" Mr. Pike was unable to preserve his air of restraint any longer, and burst forth volubly.

"That was the greatest, the most sudden, the most vital of our changes, sir - the change in the world's thought! Ideas are the real things, sir! Brick and mortar? Bah! We can put brick and mortar in any shape we choose - but we have to choose first! What held the old world back was not facts - not conditions - not any material limitations, or psychic limitations either. We had every constituent of human happiness, sir - except the sense to use them. The channel of progress was obstructed with a deposit of prehistoric ideas. We choked up our children's minds with this mental refuse as we choked our rivers and harbors with material refuse, sir."

Dr. Harkness still smiled. "Mr. Pike was in my class ten years ago," he observed amiably. "I always said he was the brightest young man I had. We are all very proud of Mr. Pike."

Mr. Pike seemed not over pleased with this communication, and the old gentleman went on:

"He is entirely right. Our idiotic ideas and theories were the main causes of poverty after all. The new views on economics - true social economics, not the "dismal science'; with the blaze of the new religion to show what was right and wrong, and the sudden uprising of half the adult world - the new voters - to carry out the new ideas; these were what changed things! There you have it, Mr. Robertson, in a nutshell - rather a large nutshell, a pericarp, as it were - but I think that covers it."

"We students used always to admire Dr. Harkness' power of easy generalization," said Mr. Pike, in a mild, subacid tone, "but if any ground of inquiry is left to you, Mr. Robertson, I could, perhaps, illuminate some special points."

Dr. Harkness laughed in high good humor, and clapped his whilom pupil on the back.

"You have the floor, Mr. Pike - I shall listen to you with edification."

The young man looked a little ashamed of his small irony, and continued more genially:

"Our first step - or one of our first steps, for we advanced like a strenuous centipede - was to check the birth of defectives and degenerates. Certain classes of criminals and perverts were rendered incapable of reproducing their kind. In the matter of those diseases most injurious to the young, very stringent measures were taken. It was made a felony to infect wife or child knowingly, and a misdemeanor if it were done unknowingly. Physicians were obliged to report all cases of infectious disease, and young girls were clearly taught the consequence of marriage with infected persons. The immediate result was, of course, a great decrease in marriage; but the increase in population was scarce checked at all because of the lowered death rate among children. It was checked a little; but for twenty years now, it has been recovering itself. We increase a little too fast now, but see every hope of a balanced population long before the resources of the world are exhausted."

Mr. Brown seized upon a second moment's pause to suggest that the world's resources were vastly increased also - and still increasing.

"Let Pike rest a moment and get his breath," he said, warming to the subject, "I want to tell Mr. Robertson that the productivity of the earth is gaining every year. Here's this old earth feeding us all - laying golden eggs as it were; and we used to get those eggs by the Caesarian operation! We uniformly exhausted the soil - uniformly! Now a man would no more think of injuring the soil, the soil that feeds him, than he would of hurting his mother. We steadily improve the soil; we improve the seed; we improve methods of culture; we improve everything."

Mrs. Allerton struck in here, "Not forgetting the methods of transportation, Mr. Robertson. There was one kind of old world folly which made great waste of labor and time; that was our constant desire to eat things out of season. There is now a truer sense of what is really good eating; no one wants to eat asparagus that is not of the best, and asparagus cut five or ten days cannot be really good. We do not carry things about unnecessarily; and the carrying we do is swift, easy and economical. For slow freight we use waterways wherever possible - you will be pleased to see the "all-water routes' that thread the country now. And our roads - you haven't seen our roads yet! We lead the world."

"We used to be at the foot of the class as to roads, did we not?" I asked; and Mr. Pike swiftly answered:

"We did, indeed, sir. But that very need of good roads made easy to us the second step in abolishing poverty. Here was a great social need calling for labor; here were thousands of men calling for employment; and here were we keeping the supply from the demand by main strength - merely from those archaic ideas of ours.

"We had a mass of valuable data already collected, and now that the whole country teemed with new ideals of citizenship and statesmanship, it did not take very long to get the two together."

"We furnished employment for all the women, too," my sister added. "A Social Service Union was formed the country over; it was part of the new religion. Every town has one - men and women. The same spirit that used to give us crusaders and missionaries now gave plenty of enthusiastic workers."

"I don't see yet how you got up any enthusiasm about work," said I.

"It was not work for oneself," Nellie explained. "That is what used to make it so sordid; we used really to believe that we were working each for himself. This new idea was overwhelming in its simplicity - and truth; work is social service - social service is religion - that's about it."

"Not only so," Dr. Harkness added, "it made a three-fold appeal; to the old, deep-seated religious sense; to the new, vivid intellectual acceptance; and to the very wide-spread, wholesome appreciation of a clear advantage.

"When a thing was offered to the world that agreed with every social instinct, that appealed to common sense, that was established by the highest scientific authority, and that had the overwhelming sanction of religion - why the world took to it."

"But it is surely not natural to people to work - much less to like to work!" I protested.

"There's where the change comes in," Mr. Pike eagerly explained. "We used to *think* that people hated work - nothing of the sort! What people hated was too much work, which is death; work they were personally unfit for and therefore disliked, which is torture; work under improper conditions, which is disease;

work held contemptible, looked down upoh by other people, which is a grievous social distress; and work so ill-paid that no human beings could really live by it."

"Why Mr. Robertson, if you can throw any light on the now inconceivable folly of that time so utterly behind us, we shall be genuinely indebted to you. It was quite understood in your day that the whole world's life, comfort, prosperity and progress depended upon the work done, was it not?"

"Why, of course; that was an economic platitude," I answered.

"Then why were the workers punished for doing it?"

"Punished? What do you mean?"

"I mean just what I say. They were punished, just as we punish criminals - with confinement at hard labor. The great mass of the people were forced to labor for cruelly long hours at dull, distasteful occupations; is not that punishment?"

"Not at all," I said hotly. "They were free at any time to leave an occupation they did not like."

Leave it for what alternative?" To take up another," said I, perceiving that this, after all, was not much of an escape.

"Yes, to take up another under the same heavy conditions, if there was any opening; or to starve - that was their freedom."

"Well, what would you have?" I asked. "A man must work for his living surely."

"Remember your economic platitude, Mr. Robertson," Dr. Harkness suggested. "The whole world's life, comfort, prosperity and progress depends upon the work done, you know. It was not *their* living they were working for; it was the world's."

"That is very pretty as a sentiment," I was beginning; but his twinkling eye reminded that an economic platitude is not precisely sentimental.

"That's where the change came," Mr. Pike eagerly repeated. "The idea that each man had to do it for himself kept us blinded to the fact that it was all social service; that they worked for the world, and the world treated them shamefully - so shamefully that their product was deteriorated, markedly deteriorated."

"You will be continually surprised, Mr. Robertson, at the improvements of our output," remarked Mr. Brown. "We have standards in every form of manufacture, required standards; and to label an article incorrectly is a misdemeanor."

"That was just starting in the pure-food agitation, you remember," my sister put in - ('with apple juice containing one-tenth of one per cent, of benzoate of soda')."

"And now," Mr. Brown continued, " 'all wool' is all wool; if it isn't, you can have the dealer arrested. Silk is silk, nowadays, and cream is cream."

"And *caveat emptor* is a dead letter?" "Yes, it is *caveat vendor* now. You see, selling goods is public service."

"You apply that term quite differently from what it stood for in my memory," said I.

"It used to mean some sort of beneficent statesmanship, at first," Nellie agreed. "Then it spread to various philanthropic efforts and wider grades of government activities. Now it means any kind of world work."

She saw that this description did not carry much weight with me, and added, "Any kind of human work, John; that is, work a man gives his whole time to and does not himself consume, is world work - is social service."

"If a man raises, by his own labor, just enough to feed himself - that is working for himself," Mr. Brown explained, "but if he raises more corn than he consumes, he is serving humanity."

"But he does not give it away," I urged; "he is paid for it."

"Well, you paid the doctor who saved your child's life, but the doctor's work was social service none the less - and the teacher's - anybody's."

"But that kind of work benefits humanity - "

"Yes, and does it not benefit humanity to eat - to have shoes and clothes and houses? John, John, wake up!" Nellie for the first time showed impatience with me. But my brother-in-law extended a protecting arm.

Now, Nellie, don't hurry him. This thing will burst upon him all at once. Of course, it's glaringly plain, but there was a time when you and I did not see it either."

I was a little sulky. "Well, as far as I gather," and I took out my note-book, "people all of a sudden changed all their ideas about everything - and your demi-millennium followed."

"I wish we *could* say that," said Mrs. Allerton. "We axe not telling you of our present day problems and difficulties, you see. No, Mr. Robertson, we have merely removed our most obvious and patently unnecessary difficulties, of which poverty was at least the largest.

"What we did, as we have rather confusedly suggested, I'm afraid, was to establish such measures as to insure better births, and vastly better environment and education for every child. That raised the standard of the people, you see, and increased their efficiency. Then we provided employment for everyone, under good conditions, and improved the world in two ways at once."

"And who paid for this universal employment?" I asked.

"Who paid for it before?" she returned promptly.

"The employer, of course."

"Did he? Out of his own private pocket? At a loss to himself."

"Why, of course not," I replied, a little nettled. "Out of the profits of the business."

"And 'the business' was the work done by the employees?"

"Not at all! He did it himself; they only furnished the labor."

"Could he do it alone - without 'labor?' Did he furnish employment as a piece of beneficence, outside of his business - Ah, Mr. Robertson, surely it is clear that unless a man's labor furnished a profit to his employer, he would not be employed. It was on that profit that 'labor' was paid - they paid themselves. They do now, but at a higher rate."

I was annoyed by this clever juggling with the hard facts of business.

"That is very convincing, Mrs. Allerton," I said with some warmth, "but it unfortunately omits certain factors. A lot of laborers could make a given article, of course; but they could not sell it - and that is where the profit comes in. What good would it do the laborer to pile up goods if he could not sell them?"

"And what good would be the ability to sell goods if there were none, Mr. Robertson. Of course, I recognize the importance of transportation; that is my own line of work, but there must be something to transport. As long ago as St. Paul's day it was known that the hand could not say to the foot, 'I have no need of thee.'"

"To cover that ground more easily, Mr. Robertson," Dr. Harkness explained, "just put down in your digest there that Bureaus of Employment were formed all over the country; some at first were of individual initiative, but in a few years' time all were in government management. There was a swift and general improvement in the whole country. The roads became models to the world, the harbors were cleared, canals dug, cities rebuilt, bare hills reforested, the value of our national property doubled and trebled - all owing to the employment of hitherto neglected labor. Out of the general increase of wealth they got their share, of course. And where there is work for everyone, at good wages, there is no poverty; that's clearly seen."

CHAPTER 7

The country was as astonishing to me as the city - its old beauty added to in every direction. They took me about in motor cars, motor boats and air ships, on foot and on horseback (the only horses now to be found were in the country). And while I speak of horses, I will add that the only dogs and cats I saw, or heard, were in the country, too, and not very numerous at that. "We've changed our views as to 'pets' and 'domestic animals,' " Nellie said. "We ourselves are the only domestic animals allowed now. Meat eating, as Hallie told you, is decreasing every day; but the care and handling of our food animals improves even more rapidly. Every city has its municipal pastures and dairies, and every village or residence group. By the way, I might as well show you one of those last, and get it clear in your mind."

We were on an air trip in one of the smooth-going, noiseless machines commonly used, which opened a new world of delight to me. This one held two, with the aviator. I had inquired about accidents, and was glad to find that thirty years' practice had eliminated the worst dangers and reared a race of flying men.

"In our educational plan today all the children are given full physical development and control," my sister explained. "That goes back to the woman again - the mothers. There was a sort of Hellenic revival - a recognition that it was possible for us to rear as beautiful human beings as walked in Athens. When women were really free of man's selective discrimination they proved quite educable, and learned to be ashamed of their deformities. Then we began to appreciate the human body and to have children reared in an atmosphere of lovely form and color, statues and pictures all about them, and the new stories - Oh! I haven't told you a thing about them, have I?"

"No," I said; "and please don't. I started out to see the country, and your new-fangled 'residence groups,' whatever they may be, and I refuse to have my mind filled up with educational information. Take me on a school expedition another time, please."

"All right," she agreed; "but I can tell you more about the beasts without distracting your mind, I hope. For one thing, we have no longer any menageries."

"What?" I cried. "No menageries!" How absurd! They were certainly educational, and a great pleasure to children - and other people."

"Our views of education have changed you see," she replied; "and our views of human relation to the animal world; also our ideas of pleasure. People do not think it a pleasure now to watch animals in pain."

"More absurdity! They were not in pain. They were treated better than when left wild," I hotly replied.

"Imprisonment is never a pleasure," she answered; "it is a terrible punishment. A menagerie is just a prison, not for any offense of the inmates, but to gratify men in the indulgence of grossly savage impulses. Children, being in the savage period of their growth, feel anew the old satisfaction of seeing their huge enemies harmless or their small victims helpless and unable to escape. But it did no human being any good."

"How about the study of these 'victims' of yours - the scientific value?"

"For such study as is really necessary to us, or to them, some laboratories keep a few. Otherwise, the student goes to where the animals live and studies their real habits."

"And how much would he learn of wild tigers by following them about - unless it was an inside view?"

"My dear brother, can you mention one single piece of valuable information for humanity to be found in the study of imprisoned tigers? As a matter of fact, I don't think there are any left by this time; I hope not."

"Do you mean to tell me that your new humanitarianism has exterminated whole species?"

"Why not? Would England be pleasant if the gray wolf still ran at large? We are now trying, as rapidly as possible, to make this world safe and habitable everywhere."

"And how about the hunting? Where's the big game?"

"Another relic of barbarism. There is very little big game left, and very little hunting."

I glared at her, speechless. Not that I was ever a hunter myself, or even wanted to be; but to have that splendid manly sport utterly prevented - it was outrageous! "I suppose this is more of the women's work," I said at length.

She cheerfully admitted it. "Yes, we did it. You see, hunting as a means of livelihood is even lower than private housework - far too wasteful and expensive to be allowed in a civilized world. When women left off using skins and feathers, that was a great blow to the industry. As to the sport, why, we had never greatly admired it, you know - the manly sport of killing things for fun - and with our new power we soon made it undesirable."

I groaned in spirit. "Do you mean to tell me that you have introduced legislation against hunting, and found means to enforce it?"

"We found means to enforce it without much legislation, John."

"As for instance?"

"As for instance, in rearing children who saw and heard the fullest condemnation of all such primitive cruelty. That is another place where the new story-books come in. Why on earth we should have fed our children on silly savagery a thousand years old, just because they liked it, is more than I can see.

We were always interfering with their likes and dislikes in other ways. Why so considerate in this? We have a lot of splendid writers now - first-class ones - making a whole lot of new literature for children."

"Do leave out your story books. You were telling me how you redoubtable females coerced men into giving up hunting."

"Mostly by disapproval, consistent and final."

This was the same sort of thing Owen had referred to in regard to tobacco. I didn't like it. It gave me a creepy feeling, as of one slowly surmounted by a rising tide. "Are you - do you mean to tell me, Nellie, that you women are trying to make men over to suit yourselves?"

"Yes. Why not? Didn't you make women to suit yourselves for several thousand years? You bred and trained us to suit your tastes; you liked us small, you liked us weak, you liked us timid, you liked us ignorant, you liked us pretty - what you called pretty - and you eliminated the kinds you did not like."

"How, if you please?"

"By the same process we use - by not marrying them. Then, you see, there aren't any more of that kind."

"You are wrong, Nellie - you're absurdly wrong. Women were naturally that way; that is, womanly women were, and men preferred that kind, of course."

"How do you know women were 'naturally' like that? - without special education and artificial selection, and all manner of restrictions and penalties? Where were any women ever allowed to grow up 'naturally' until now?"

I maintained a sulky silence, looking down at the lovely green fields and forests beneath. "Have you exterminated dogs?" I asked.

"Not yet. There are a good many real dogs left. But we don't make artificial ones any more."

"I suppose you keep all the cats - being women." She laughed.

"No; we keep very few. Cats kill birds, and we need the birds for our farms and gardens. They keep the insects down."

"Do they keep the mice down, too?"

"Owls and night-hawks do, as far as they can. But we attend to the mice ourselves. Concrete construction and the removal of the kitchen did that. We do not live in food warehouses now. There, look! We are coming to Westholm Park; that was one of the first."

In all the beauty spread below me, the great park showed more beautiful, outlined by a thick belt of trees.

We kept our vehicle gliding slowly above it while Nellie pointed things out. "It's about 300 acres," she said. "You can see the woodland and empty part - all that is left wild. That big patch there is pasturage

— they keep their own sheep and cows. There are gardens and meadows. Up in the corner is the children's playground, bathing pool, and special buildings. Here is the playground for grown-ups - and their lake. This big spreading thing is the guest house and general playhouse for the folks - ballroom, billiards, bowling, and so on. Behind it is the plant for the whole thing. The water tower you'll see to more advantage when we land. And all around you see the homes; each family has an acre or so."

We dropped softly to the landing platform and came down to the pleasure ground beneath. In a little motor we ran about the place for awhile, that I might see the perfect roads, shaded with arching trees, the endless variety of arrangement, the miles of flowers, the fruit on every side.

"You must have had a good landscape architect to plan this," I suggested.

"We did - one of the best."

"It's not so very unlike a great, first-class summer hotel, with singularly beautiful surroundings."

"No, it's not," she agreed. "We had only best summer resorts in mind when we began to plan these places. People used to pay heavily in summer to enjoy a place where everything was done to make life smooth and pleasant. It occurred to us at last that we might live that way."

"Who wants to live in a summer hotel all the time? Excuse *me*!"

"O, they don't. The people here nearly all live in 'homes' - the homiest kind - each on its own ground, as you see. Only some unattached ones, and people who really like it, live in the hotel - with transients, of course. Let's call here; I know this family."

She introduced me to Mrs. Masson, a sweet, motherly little woman, rocking softly on her vine-shadowed piazza, a child in her arms. She was eager to tell me about things - most people were, I found.

"I'm a reactionary, Mr. Robertson. I prefer to work at home, and I prefer to keep my children with me, all I can."

"Isn't that allowed nowadays?"I inquired.

"O, yes; if one qualifies. I did. I took the child-culture course, but I do not want to be a regular teacher. My work is done right here, and I can have them as well as not, but they won't stay much."

Even as she spoke the little thing in her arms whispered eagerly to her mother, slipped to the floor, ran out of the gate, her little pink legs fairly twinkling, and joined an older child who was passing.

"They like to be with the others, you see. This is my baby; I manage to hold on to her for part of the day, but she's always running off to The Garden when she can."

"The Garden?"

"Yes; it's a regular Child Garden, where they are cultivated and grow! And they do so love to grow!"

She showed us her pretty little house and her lovely work - embroidery. "I'm so fortunate," she said, "loving home as I do, to have work that's just as well done here."

I learned that there were some thirty families living in the grounds, not counting the hotel people. Quite a number found their work in the necessary activities of the place itself.

"We have a long string of places, you see - from the general manager to the gardeners and dairymen. It is really quite a piece of work, to care for some two hundred and fifty people," Mrs. Masson explained with some pride.

"Instead of a horde of servants and small tradesmen to make a living off these thirty families, we have a small corps of highly trained officers," added Nellie.

"And do you cooperate in housekeeping?" I inquired, meaning no harm, though my sister was quite severe with me for this slip.

"No, *indeed*," protested Mrs. Masson. "I do despise being mixed up with other families. I've been here nearly a year, and I hardly know anyone." And she rocked back and forth, complacently.

"But I thought that the meals were cooperative."

"O, not at *all* - not at *all*. Just see my dining-room! And you must be tired and hungry, now, Mrs. Robertson - don't say no! I'll have lunch in a moment. Excuse pie, please."

She retired to the telephone, but we could hear her ordering lunch. "Right away, please; No. 5; no, let me see - No. 7, please. And have you fresh mushrooms? Extra; four plates."

Her husband came home in time for the meal, and she presided just like any other little matron over a pretty table and a daintily served lunch; but it came down from the hotel in a neat, light case, to which the remnants and the dishes were returned.

"O, I wouldn't give up my own table for the world! And my own dishes; they take excellent care of them. Our breakfasts we get all together - see my kitchen!" And she proudly exhibited a small, light closet, where an immaculate porcelain sink, with hot and cold water, a glass-doored "cold closet" and a shining electric stove, allowed the preparation of many small meals.

Nellie smiled blandly as she saw this little lady claiming conservatism in what struck me as being quite sufficiently progressive, while Mr. Masson smiled in proud content.

"I took you there on purpose," she told me later. "She is really quite reactionary for nowadays, and not over popular. Come and see the guest-house."

This was a big, wide-spread concrete building, with terraces and balconies and wide roofs, where people strolled and sat. It rose proudly from its wide lawns and blooming greenery, a picture of peace and pleasure.

"It's like a country club, with more sleeping rooms," I suggested. "But isn't it awfully expensive - the year round?"

"It's about a third cheaper than it would cost these people to live if they kept house. Funny! It took nearly twenty years to prove that organization in housekeeping paid, like any other form of organized labor. Wages have risen, all the work is better done and it costs much less. You can see all that. But what you can't possibly realize is the difference it makes to women. All the change the men feel is in better food, no fret and worry at home, and smaller bills."

"That's something," I modestly suggested.

"Yes, that's a good deal; but to the women it's a thousand times more. The women who liked that kind of work are doing it now, as a profession, for reasonable hours and excellent salaries; and the women who did not like it are now free to do the work they are fitted for and enjoy. This is one of our great additions to the world's wealth - freeing so much productive energy. It has improved our health, too. One of the worst causes of disease is mal-position, you know. Almost everybody used to work at what they did not like - and we thought it was beneficial to character!"

I tried without prejudice to realize the new condition, but a house without a house-wife, without children, without servants, seemed altogether empty. Nellie reassured me as to the children, however.

"It's no worse than when they went to school, John, not a bit. If you were here at about 9 A. M., you'd see the mothers taking a morning walk, or ride if it's stormy, to the child-garden, and leaving the babies there, asleep mostly. There are seldom more than five or six real little ones at one time in a group like this."

"Do mothers leave their nursing babies there?"

"Sometimes; it depends on the kind of work they do. Remember they only have to work two hours, and many mothers get ahead on their work and take a year off at baby time. Still, two hours work a day that one enjoys, does not hurt even a nursing mother."

I found it extremely difficult from the first, to picture a world whose working day was but two hours long; or even the four hours they told me was generally given.

"What do people do with the rest of their time; working people, I mean?" I asked.

"The old ones usually rest a good deal, loaf, visit one another, play games, in some cases they travel. Others, who have the working habit ingrained, keep on in the afternoon; in their gardens often; almost all old people love gardening; and those who wish, have one now, you see. The city ones do an astonishing amount of reading, studying, going to lectures, and the theatres. They have a good time."

"But I mean the low rowdy common people - don't they merely loaf and get drunk?"

Nellie smiled at me good humoredly.

"Some of them did, for a while. But it became increasingly difficult to get drunk. You see, their health was better, with sweeter homes, better food and more pleasure; and except for the dipsomaniacs they improved in their tastes presently. Then their children all made a great advance, under the new educational methods; the women had an immense power as soon as they were independent; and between the children's influence and the woman's *and* the new opportunities, the worst men had to grow better. There was always more recuperative power in people than they were given credit for."

"But surely there were thousands, hundreds of thousands, of hoboes and paupers; wretched, degenerate creatures."

Nellie grew sober. "Yes, there were. One of our inherited handicaps was that great mass of wreckage left over from the foolishness and ignorance of the years behind us. But we dealt very thoroughly with them. As I told you before, hopeless degenerates were promptly and mercifully removed. A large class of perverts were incapacitated for parentage and placed where they could do no harm, and could still have some usefulness and some pleasure. Many proved curable, and were cured. And for the helpless residue; blind and crippled through no fault of their own, a remorseful society provides safety, comfort and care; with all the devices for occupation and enjoyment that our best minds could arrange. These are our remaining asylums; decreasing every year. We don't make that kind of people any more."

We talked as we strolled about, or sat on the stone benches under rose bush or grape vine. The beauty of the place grew on me irresistibly. Each separate family could do as they liked in their own yard, under some restriction from the management in regard to general comfort and beauty. I was always ready to cry out about interference with personal rights; but my sister reminded me that we were not allowed to "commit a nuisance" in the old days, only our range of objections had widened. A disagreeable noise is now prohibited, as much as a foul smell; and conspicuously ugly forms and colors, also.

"And who decides - who's your dictator and censor?"

"Our best judges - we elect, recall and change them. But under their guidance we have developed some general sense of beauty. People would complain loudly now of what did not use to trouble them at all."

Then I remembered that I had seen no row of wooden cows in the green meadows, no invitation to "meet me at the fountain," no assailing finger to assure me that my credit was good, no gross cathartic reminders, nothing anywhere to mar the beauty of the landscape; but many a graceful gate, temple-like summer houses crowning the grassy hills, arbors, pergolas, cool seats by stone-rimmed fountains, signs everywhere of the love of beauty and the power to make it.

"I don't see yet how you ever manage to pay for all this extra work everywhere. I suppose in a place like this it comes out of the profit made on food," I suggested.

"No - the gardening expenses of these home clubs come out of the rent."

"And what rent do they have to pay - approximately?"

"I can tell you exactly about this place, because it was opened by a sort of stock company of women, and I was in it for a while. The land cost $100.00 an acre then - $30,000.00. To get it in shape cost $10,000.00, to build thirty of these houses about $4,000.00 apiece - there was great saving in doing it all at one time, the guest-house, furnished, was only $50,000.00, it is very simple, you see; and the general plant and child-garden, and everything else, some $40,000.00 more. I know we raised a capital of $250,000.00, and used it all. The residents pay $600.00 a year for house-rent and $100.00 more for club privileges. That is $28,000.00. We take 4 per cent, and it leaves plenty for taxes and up-keep. Those who have children keep up the child-garden. The hotel makes enough to keep everything going easily, and the food and service departments pay handsomely. Why, if these people had kept on living in New York, it would have cost them altogether at least $8,000.00 a year. Here it just costs them about $2,000.00 - and just see what they get for it."

I had an inborn distrust of my sister's figures, and consulted Owen later; also Hallie, who had much detailed knowledge on the subject; and furthermore I did some reading.

There was no doubt about it. The method of living of which we used to be so proud, for which I still felt a deep longing, was abominably expensive. Much smaller amounts, wisely administered, produced better living, and for the life of me I could not discover the cackling herds of people I had been led to expect when such "Utopian schemes" used to be discussed in my youth.

From the broad, shady avenues of this quiet place we looked over green hedges or wire fences thick with honeysuckle and rose, into pleasant homelike gardens where families sat on broad piazzas, swung in hammocks, played tennis, ball, croquet, tether-ball and badminton, just as families used to.

Groups of young girls or young men - or both - strolled under the trees and disported themselves altogether as I remembered them to have done, and happy children frolicked about in the houses and gardens, all the more happily, it would appear, because they had their own place for part of the day.

We had seen the fathers come home in time for the noon meal. In the afternoon most of the parents seemed to think it the finest thing in the world to watch their children learning or playing together, in that amazing Garden of theirs, or to bring them home for more individual companionship. As a matter of fact, I had never seen, in any group of homes that I could recall, so much time given to children by so many parents - unless on a Sunday in the suburbs.

I was very silent on the way back, revolving these things in my mind. Point by point it seemed so vividly successful, so plainly advantageous, so undeniably enjoyed by those who lived there; and yet the old objections surged up continually.

The "noisy crowd all herding together to eat!" - I remembered Mr. Masson's quiet dining-room - they all had dining-rooms, it appeared. The "dreadful separation of children from their parents!" I thought of all those parents watching with intelligent interest their children's guarded play, or enjoying their companionship at home.

The "forced jumble with disagreeable neighbors!" I recalled those sheltered quiet grounds; each house with its trees and lawn, its garden and its outdoor games.

It was against all my habits, principles, convictions, theories, and sentiments; but there it was, and they seemed to like it. Also, Owen assured me, it paid.

CHAPTER 8

After all, it takes time for a great change in world-thought to strike in. That's what Owen insisted on calling it. He maintained that the amazing up-rush of these thirty years was really due to the wholesale acceptance and application of the idea of evolution.

"I don't know which to call more important - the new idea, or the new power to use it," he said. "When we were young, practically all men of science accepted the evolutionary theory of life; and it was in general popular favor, though little understood. But the governing ideas of all our earlier time were so completely out of touch with life; so impossible of any useful application, that the connection between belief and behavior was rusted out of us. Between our detached religious ideas and our brutal ignorance of brain culture, we had made ourselves preternaturally inefficient.

"Then - you remember the talk there was about Mental Healing - 'Power in Repose' - 'The Human Machine' - or was that a bit later? Anyway, people had begun to waken up to the fact that they could do things with their brains. At first they used them only to cure diseases, to maintain an artificial 'peace of mind,' and tricks like that. Then it suddenly burst upon us - two or three important books came along nearly at once, and hosts of articles - that we could use this wonderful mental power every day, to live with! That all these scientific facts and laws had an application to life - human life."

I nodded appreciatively. I was getting quite fond of my brother-in-law. We were in a small, comfortable motor boat, gliding swiftly and noiselessly up the beautiful Hudson. Its blue cleanness was a joy. I could see fish - real fish - in the clear water when we were still.

The banks were one long succession of gardens, palaces, cottages and rich woodlands, charming to view.

"It's the *time* that puzzles me more than anything," I said, "even more than the money. How on earth so much could be done in so little time!"

"That's because you conceive of it as being done in one place after another, instead of in every place at once," Owen replied. "If one city, in one year, could end the smoke nuisance, so could all the cities on earth, if they chose to. We chose to, all over the country, practically at once."

"But you speak of evolution. Evolution is the slowest of slow processes. It took us thousands of dragging years to evolve the civilization of 1910, and you show me a 1940 that seems thousands of years beyond that."

"Yes; but what you call Evolution' was that of unaided nature. Social evolution is a distinct process. Below us, you see, all improvements had to be built into the stock - transmitted by heredity. The social organism is open to lateral transmission - what we used to call education. We never understood it. We thought it was to supply certain piles of information, mostly useless; or to develop certain qualities."

"And what do you think it is now?" I asked.

"We know now that *the* social process is to constantly improve and develop society. This has a necessary corollary of improvement in individuals; but the thing that matters most is growth in the social spirit - and body."

"You're beyond me now, Owen."

"Yes; don't you notice that ever since you began to study our advance, what puzzles you most is not the visible details about you, but a changed spirit in people? Thirty years ago, if you showed a man that some one had dumped a ton of soot in his front yard he would have been furious, and had the man arrested and punished. If you showed him that numbers of men were dumping thousands of tons of soot all over his city every year, he would hiave neither felt nor acted. It's the other way, now."

"You speak as if man had really learned to 'love his neighbor as himself,'" I said sarcastically.

"And why not? If you have a horse, on whose strength you absolutely depend to make a necessary journey, you take good care of that horse and grow fond of him. It dawned on us at last that life was not an individual affair; that other people were essential to our happiness - to our very existence. We are not what they used to call 'altruistic' in this. We do not think of 'neighbors,' 'brothers,' 'others' any more. It is all 'ourself.'"

"I don't follow you - sorry."

Owen grinned at me amiably. "No matter, old chap, you can see results, and will have to take the reasons on trust. Now here's this particular river with its natural beauties, and its unnatural defilements. We simply stopped defiling it - and one season's rain did the rest."

"Did the rains wash away the rail-roads?"

"Oh, no - they are there still. But the use of electric power has removed the worst evils. There is no smoke, dust, cinders, and a yearly saving of millions in forest fires on the side! Also very little noise. Come and see the way it works now."

We ran in at Yonkers. I wouldn't have known the old town. It was as beautiful as - Posilippo."

"Where are the factories?" I asked.

"There - and there - and there."

"Why, those are palaces!"

"Well? Why not? Why shouldn't people work in palaces? It doesn't cost any more to make a beautiful building than an ugly one. Remember, we are much richer, now - and have plenty of time, and the spirit of beauty is encouraged."

I looked at the rows of quiet, stately buildings; wide-windowed, garden-roofed.

"Electric power there too?" I suggested.

Owen nodded again. "Everywhere," he said. "We store electricity all the time with wind-mills, water-mills, tide-mills, solar engines - even hand power."

"What!"

"I mean it," he said. "There are all kinds of storage batteries now. Huge ones for mills, little ones for houses; and there are ever so many people whose work does not give them bodily exercise, and who do not care much for games. So we have both hand and foot attachments; and a vigorous man, or woman - or child, for that matter, can work away for half an hour, and have the pleasant feeling that the power used will heat the house or run the motor."

"Is that why I don't smell gasoline in the streets?"

"Yes. We use all those sloppy, smelly things in special places - and apply all the power by electric storage mostly. You saw the little batteries in our boat."

Then he showed me the railroad. There were six tracks, clean and shiny - thick turf between them.

"The inside four are for the special trains - rapid transit and long distance freight. The outside two are open to anyone."

We stopped long enough to see some trains go by; the express at an incredible speed, yet only buzzing softly; and the fast freight; cars seemingly of aluminum, like a string of silver beads.

"We use aluminum for almost everything. You know it was only a question of power - the stuff is endless," Owen explained.

And all the time, on the outside tracks, which had a side track at every station, he told me, ran single coaches or short trains, both passenger and freight, at a comfortable speed.

"All kinds of regular short-distance traffic runs this way. It's a great convenience. But the regular highroads are the best. Have you noticed?"

I had seen from the air-motor how broad and fine they looked, but told him I had made no special study of them.

"Come on - while we're about it," he said; and called a little car. We ran up the hills to Old Broadway, and along its shaded reaches for quite a distance. It was broad, indeed. The center track, smooth, firm, and dustless, was for swift traffic of any sort, and well used. As the freight wagons were beautiful to look at and clean, they were not excluded, and the perfect road was strong enough for any load. There were rows of trees on either side, showing a good growth, though young yet; then a narrower roadway for slower vehicles, on either side a second row of trees, the footpaths, and the outside trees.

"These are only about twenty-five years old. Don't you think they are doing well?"

"They are a credit to the National Bureau of Highways and Arboriculture that I see you are going to tell me about."

"You *are* getting wise," Owen answered, with a smile. "Yes - that's what does it. And it furnishes employment, I can tell you. In the early morning these roads are alive with caretakers. Of course the bulk of the work is done by running machines; but there is a lot of pruning and trimming and fighting with insects. Among our richest victories in that line is the extermination of the gipsy moth - brown tail - elm beetle and the rest."

"How on earth did you do that?"

"Found the natural devourer - as we did with the scale pest. Also by raising birds instead of killing them; and by swift and thorough work in the proper season. We gave our minds to it, you see, at last."

The outside path was a delightful one, wide, smooth, soft to the foot, agreeable in color.

"What do you make your sidewalk of?" I asked.

Owen tapped it with his foot. "It's a kind of semi-flexible concrete - wears well, too. And we color it to suit ourselves, you see. There was no real reason why a path should be ugly to look at."

Every now and then there were seats; also of concrete, beautifully shaped and too heavy to be easily moved. A narrow crack ran along the lowest curve.

"That keeps 'em dry," said Owen.

Drinking fountains bubbled invitingly up from graceful standing basins, where birds drank and dipped in the overflow.

"Why, these are fruit trees," I said suddenly, looking along the outside row.

"Yes, nearly all of them, and the next row are mostly nut trees. You see, the fruit trees are shorter and don't take the sun off. The middle ones are elms wherever elms grow well. I tell you, John, it is the experience of a lifetime to take a long motor trip over the roads of America! You can pick your climate, or run with the season. Nellie and I started once from New Orleans in February - the violets out. We came north with them; I picked her a fresh bunch every day!"

He showed me the grape vines trained from tree to tree in Tuscan fashion; the lines of berry bushes, and the endless ribbon of perennial flowers that made the final border of the pathway. On its inner side were beds of violets, lilies of the valley, and thick ferns; and around each fountain were groups of lilies and water-loving plants.

I shook my head.

"I don't believe it," I said. "I *simply don't believe it*! How could any nation afford to keep up such roads!"

Owen drew me to a seat - we had dismounted to examine a fountain and see the flowers. He produced pencil and paper.

"I'm no expert," he said. "I can't give you exact figures. But I want you to remember that the trees pay. Pay! These roads, hundreds of thousands of miles of them, constitute quite a forest, and quite an orchard. Nuts, as Hallie told you, are in growing use as food. We have along these roads, as beautiful clean shade trees, the finest improved kinds of chestnut, walnut, butternut, pecan - whatever grows best in the locality."

And then he made a number of startling assertions and computations, and showed me the profit per mile of two rows of well-kept nut trees.

"I suppose Hallie has told you about tree farming?" he added.

"She said something about it - but I didn't rightly know what she meant."

"Oh, it's a big thing; it has revolutionized agriculture. As you're sailing over the country now you don't see so many bald spots. A healthy, permanent world has to keep its fur on."

I was impressed by that casual remark, "As you're sailing over the country."

"Look here, Owen, I think I have the glimmer of an idea. Didn't the common use of airships help to develop this social consciousness you're always talking about - this general view of things?"

He clapped me on the shoulder. "You're dead right, John - it did, and I don't believe any of us would have thought to mention it." He looked at me admiringly. "Behold the power of a naturally strong mind - in spite of circumstances! Yes, really that's a fact. You see few people are able to visualize what they have not seen. Most of us had no more idea of the surface of the earth than an ant has of a meadow. In each mind was only a thready fragment of an idea of the world - no real geographic *view*. And when we got flying all over it commonly, it became real and familiar to us - like a big garden.

"I guess that helped on the tree idea. You see, in our earlier kind of agriculture the first thing we did was to cut down the forest, dig up and burn over, plow, harrow, and brush fine - to plant our little grasses. All that dry, soft, naked soil was helplessly exposed to the rain - and the rain washed it steadily away. In one heavy storm soil that it had taken centuries of forest growth to make would be carried off to clog the rivers and harbors. This struck us all at once as wasteful. We began to realize that food could grow on trees as well as grasses; that the cubic space occupied by a chestnut tree could produce more bushels of nutriment than the linear space below it. Of course we have our wheat fields yet, but around every exposed flat acreage is a broad belt of turf and trees; every river and brook is broadly bordered with turf and trees, or shrubs. We have stopped soil waste to a very great extent. Also we make soil - but that is a different matter."

"Hurrying Mother Nature again, eh?"

"Yes, the advance in scientific agriculture is steady. Don't you remember that German professor who raised all kinds of things in water? Just fed them a pinch of chemicals now and then? They said he had a row of trees before his door with their roots in barrels of water - the third generation that had never touched ground. We kept on studying, and began to learn how to put together the proper kind of soil for different kinds of plants. Rock-crushers furnished the basis, then add the preferred constituents and sell, by the bag or the ship load. You can have a radish bed in a box on your window sill, if you like radishes, that will raise you the fattest, sweetest, juiciest, crispiest, tenderest little pink beauties you ever saw - all the year round. No weed seeds in that soil, either."

We rolled slowly back in the green shade. There was plenty of traffic, but all quiet, orderly, and comfortable. The people were a constant surprise to me. They were certainly better looking, even the poorest. And on the faces of the newest immigrants there was an expression of blazing hope that was almost better than the cheery peacefulness of the native born.

Wherever I saw workmen, they worked swiftly, with eager interest. Nowhere did I see the sagging slouch, the slow drag of foot and dull swing of arm which I had always associated with day laborers. We saw men working in the fields - and women, too; but I had learned not to lay my neck on the block too frequently. I knew that my protest would only bring out explanations of the advantage of field work over house work - and that women were as strong as men - or thereabouts. But I was surprised at their eagerness.

"They look as busy as a lot of ants on an ant heap," I said.

"It's their heap, you see," Owen answered. "And they are not tired - that makes a great difference."

"They seem phenomenally well dressed - looks like a scene in an opera. Sort of agricultural uniform?"

"Why not?" Owen was always asking me "why not" - and there wasn't any answer to it. "We used to have hunting suits and fishing suits and plumbing suits, and so on. It isn't really a uniform, just the natural working out of the best appointed dress for the trade."

Again I held my tongue; not asking how they could afford it, but remembering the shorter hours, the larger incomes, the more universal education.

We got back to Yonkers, put up the car - these things could be hired, I found, for twenty-five cents an hour - and had lunch in a little eating place which bore out Hallie's statement as to the high standard of food everywhere. Our meal was twenty-five cents for each of us. I saw Owen smile at me, but I refused to be surprised. We settled down in our boat again, and pushed smoothly up the river.

"I wish you'd get one thing clear in my mind," I said at last. "Just how did you tackle the liquor question. I haven't seen a saloon - or a drunken man. Nellie said something about people's not wanting to drink any more - but there were several millions who did want to, thirty years ago, and plenty of people who wanted them to. What were your steps?"

"The first step was to eliminate the self-interest of the dealer - the big business pressure that had to make drunkards. That was done in state after state, within a few years, by introducing government ownership and management. With that went an absolute government guarantee of purity. In five or six years there was no bad liquor sold, and no public drinking places except government ones.

"But that wasn't enough - not by a long way. It wasn't the love of liquor that supported the public house - it was the need of the public house itself."

I stared rather uncertainly,

"The meeting place," he went on. "Men have to get together. We have had public houses as long as we have had private ones, almost. It is a social need."

"A social need with a pretty bad result, it seems to me," I said, "that took men away from their families, leading to all manner of vicious indulgence."

"Yes, they used to; but that was because only men used them. I said a social need, not a masculine one. We have met it in this way. Whenever we build private houses - if it is the lowest country unit, or the highest city block, we build accommodations for living together.

"Every little village has its Town House, with club rooms of all sorts; the people flock together freely, for games, for talk, for lectures, and plays, and dances, and sermons - it is universal. And in the city - you don't see a saloon on every corner, but you do see almost as many places where you can 'meet a man' and talk with him on equal ground."

"Meet a woman, too?" I suggested.

"Yes; especially, yes. People can meet, as individuals or in groups, freely and frequently, in city or country. But men can not flock by themselves in special places provided for their special vices - without taking a great deal of extra trouble."

"I should think they would take the trouble, then," said I.

"But why? When there is every arrangement made for a natural good time; when you are not overworked, not underfed, not miserable and hopeless. When you can drop into a comfortable chair and have excellent food and drink in pleasant company; and hear good music, or speaking, or reading, or see pictures; or, if you like, play any kind of game; swim, ride, fly, do what you want to, for change and recreation - why long for liquor in a low place?"

"But the men - the real men, people as they were," I insisted. "You had a world full of drinking men who liked the saloon; did you - what do you call it? - eliminate them?"

A few of them, yes," he replied gravely; Some preferred it; others, thorough-going dipsomaniacs, we gave hospital treatment and permanent restraint; they lived and worked and were well provided for in places where there was no liquor. But there were not many of that kind. Most men drank under a constant pressure of conditions driving them to it, and the mere force of habit.

"Just remember that the weight and terror of life is lifted off us - for good and all."

"Socialism, you mean?"

"Yes, real socialism. The wealth and power of all of us belongs to all of us now. The Wolf is dead."

"Other things besides poverty drove a man to drink in my time," I ventured.

"Oh, yes - and some men continued to drink. I told you there was liquor to be had - good liquor, too. And other drug habits held on for a while. But we stopped the source of the trouble. The old men died off, the younger ones got over it, and the new ones - that's what you don't realize yet: We make a new kind of people now."

He was silent, his strong mouth set in a kind smile, his eyes looking far up the blue river.

"Well, what comes next? What's done it?" I demanded. "Religion, education, or those everlasting women?"

He laughed outright; laughed till the boat rocked, "How you do hate to admit that it's their turn. John! Haven't we had full swing - everything in our hands - for all historic time? They have only begun. Thirty years? Why, John, they have done so much in these thirty years that the world's heart is glad at last. You don't know. "

I didn't know. But I did feel a distinct resentment at being treated like an extinct species.

"They have simply stepped on to an eminence men have been all these years building," I said. "We have done all the hard work - are doing it yet, for all I see. We have made it possible for them to live at all! We have made the whole civilization of the world - they just profit by it. And now you speak as if, somehow, they had managed to achieve more than we have!"

Owen considered a while thoughtfully. "What you say is true. We have done a good deal of the work; we did largely make and modify our civilization. But if you read some of the newer histories " he stopped and looked at me as if I had just happened. "Why you don't know yet, do you? History has been rewritten."

"You speak as if 'history' was a one act play."

"I don't mean it's all done, of course - but we do have now a complete new treatment of the world's history. Each nation its own, some several of them, there's no dead level of agreement, I assure you. But our old androcentric version of life began to be questioned about 1910, I think - and new versions appeared, more and more of them. The big scholars took it up, there was new research work, and now we are not so glib in our assurance that we did it all."

"You're getting pretty close to things I used to know something about," I remarked drily.

"If you knew all that was known, then, you wouldn't know this, John. Don't you remember what Lester Ward calls 'the illusion of the near' - how the most familiar facts were precisely those we often failed to understand? In all our history, ancient and modern, we had the underlying asumption that men were the human race, the people who did things; and that women - were 'their women.' "

And precisely what have you lately discovered? That Horatio at the bridge was Horatia, after all? That the world was conquered by an Alexandra - and a Napoleona?" I laughed with some bitterness.

"No," said Owen gently, "There is no question about the battles - men did the fighting, of course. But we have learned that 'the decisive battles of history' were not so decisive as we thought them. Man, as a destructive agent did modify history, unquestionably. What did make history, make civilization, was constructive industry. And for many ages women did most of that."

"Did women build the Pyramids? the Acropolis? the Roads of Rome?"

"No, nor many other things. But they gave the world its first start in agriculture and the care of animals; they clothed it and fed it and ornamented it and kept it warm; their ceaseless industry made rich the simple early cultures. Consider - without men, Egypt and Assyria could not have fought - but they could have grown rich and wise. Without women - they could have fought until the last man died alone - if the food held out.

"But I won't bother you with this, John. You'll get all you want out of books better than I can give it. What I set out to say was that the most important influence in weeding out intemperance was that of the women."

I was in a very bad temper by this time, it was disagreeable enough to have this - or any other part of it, true; but what I could not stand was to see that big hearted man speak of it in such a cheerful matter-of-fact way.

"Have the men of today no pride?" I asked. "How can you stand it - being treated as inferiors - by women?"

"Women stood it for ten thousand years," he answered, "being treated as inferiors - by men."

We went home in silence.

CHAPTER 9

I learned to understand the immense material prosperity of the country much more easily than its social progress.

The exquisite agriculture which made millions of acres from raw farms and ranches into rich gardens, the forestry which had changed our straggling woodlands into great tree-farms, yielding their steady crops of cut boughs, thinned underbrush, and full-grown trunks, those endless orchard roads, with their processions of workers making continual excursions in their special cars, keeping roadway and bordering trees in perfect order - all this one could see.

There were, of course far more of the wilder, narrower roads, perfect as the road-bed, but not parked, with all untrimmed nature to travel through.

The airships did make a difference. To look down on the flowing, outspread miles beneath gave a sense of the unity and continuous beauty of our country, quite different from the streak views we used to get. An airship is a moving mountain-top.

The cities were even more strikingly beautiful, in that the change was greater, the contrast sharper. I never tired of wandering about on foot along the streets of cities, and I visited several, finding, as Nellie said, that it took no longer to improve twenty than one; the people in each could do it as soon as they chose to.

But what made them choose? What had got into the people? That was what puzzled me most. It did not show outside, like the country changes, and the rebuilt cities; the people did not look remarkable, though they were different, too. I watched and studied them, trying to analyze the changes that could be seen. Most visible was cleanliness, comfort, and beauty in dress.

I had never dreamed of the relief to the spectator in not seeing any poverty. We were used to it, of course; we had our excuses, religious and economic, we even found, or thought we found, artistic pleasure in this social disease. But now I realized what a nightmare it had been - the sights, the sounds, the smells of poverty - merely to an outside observer.

These people had good bodies, too. They were not equally beautiful, by any means; thirty years, of course, could not wholly return to the normal a race long stunted and overworked. But in the difference in the young generation I could see at a glance the world's best hope, that the "long inheritance" is far deeper than the short.

Those of about twenty and under, those who were born after some of these changes had been made, were like another race. Big, sturdy, blooming creatures, boys and girls alike, swift and graceful, eager, happy, courteous - I supposed at first that these were the children of exceptionally placed people; but soon found, with a heart-stirring sort of shock, that all the children were like that.

Some of the old folk still carried the scars of earlier conditions, but the children were new people.

Then of my own accord I demanded reasons. Nellie laughed sweetly.

"I'm so glad you've come to your appetite," she said. "I've been longing to talk to you about that, and you were always bored."

"It's a good deal of a dose, Nell; you'll admit that. And one hates to be forcibly fed. But now I do want to get an outline, a sort of general idea, of what you do with children. Can you condense a little recent history, and make it easy to an aged stranger?"

"Aged! You are growing younger every day, John. I believe that comparatively brainless life you led in Tibet was good for you. That was all new impression on the brain; the first part rested. Now you are beginning where you left off. I wish you would recognize that."

I shook my head. "Never mind me, I'm trying not to think of my chopped-off life; but tell me how you manufacture this kind of people."

My sister sat still, thinking, for a little. "I want to avoid repetition if possible - tell me just how much you have in mind already." But I refused to be catechised.

"You put it all together, straight; I want to get the whole of it - as well as I can."

"All right. On your head be it. Let me see - first. Oh, there isn't any first, John! We were doing ever so much for children before you left - before you and I were born! It is the vision of all the great child-lovers; that children are people, and the most valuable people on earth. The most important thing to a child is its mother. We made new mothers for them - I guess that is 'first.'

"Suppose we begin this way:

"a. Free, healthy, independent, intelligent mothers.

"b. Enough to live on - right conditions for child-raising.

"c. Specialized care.

"d. The new social consciousness, with its religion, its art, its science, its civics, its industry, its wealth, its brilliant efficiency. That's your outline."

I set down these points in my note-book.

"An excellent outline, Nellie. Now for details on 'a.' I will set my teeth till that's over."

My sister regarded me with amused tenderness. "How you do hate the new women, John - in the abstract! I haven't seen you averse to any of them in the concrete!"

At the time I refused to admit any importance to this remark, but I thought it over later - and to good purpose. It was true. I did hate the new kind of human being who loomed so large in every line of progress. She jarred on every age-old masculine prejudice - she was not what woman used to be. And yet - as Nellie said - the women I met I liked.

"Get on with the lesson, my dear," said I. "I am determined to learn and not to argue. What did your omnipresent new woman do to improve the human stock so fast?"

Then Nellie settled down in earnest and gave me all I wanted - possibly more.

"They wakened as if to a new idea, to their own natural duty as mothers; to the need of a high personal standard of health and character in both parents. That gave us a better start right away - clean-born, vigorous children, inheriting strength and purity.

"Then came the change in conditions, a change so great you've hardly glimpsed it yet. No more, never more again, please God, that brutal hunger and uncertainty, that black devil of want and fear. Everybody - everybody - sure of decent living! That one thing lifted the heaviest single shadow from the world, and from the children.

"Nobody is overworked now. Nobody is tired, unless they tire themselves unnecessarily. People live sanely, safely, easily. The difference to children, both in nature and nurture, is very great. They all have proper nourishment, and clothing, and environment - from birth.

"And with that, as advance in special conditions for child-culture, we build for babies now. We, as a community, provide suitably for our most important citizens."

At this point I opened my mouth to say something, but presently shut it again.

"Good boy!" said Nellie. "I'll show you later."

"The next is specialized care. That one thing is enough, almost, to account for it all. To think of all the ages when our poor babies had no benefit at all of the advance in human intelligence!

"We had the best and wisest specialists we could train and hire in every other field of life - and the babies left utterly at the mercy of amateurs!

"Well, I mustn't stop to rage at past history. We do better now. John, guess the salary of the head of the Baby Gardens in a city."

"Oh, call it a million, and go on," I said cheerfully; which somewhat disconcerted her.

"It's as big a place as being head of Harvard College," she said, "and better paid than that used to be. Our highest and finest people study for this work. Real geniuses, some of them. The babies, all the babies, mind you, get the benefit of the best wisdom we have. And it grows fast. We are learning by doing it. Every year we do better. 'Growing up' is an easier process than it used to be."

"I'll have to accept it for the sake of argument," I agreed. "It's the last point I care most for, I think. All these new consciousnesses you were so glib about. I guess you can't describe that so easily."

She grew thoughtful, rocking to and fro for a few moments.

"No," she said at length, "it's not so easy. But I'll try. I wasn't very glib, really. I spoke of religion, art, civics, science, industry, wealth, and efficiency, didn't I? Now let's see how they apply to the children."

"This religion. Dear me, John! am I to explain the greatest sunburst of truth that that ever was - in two minutes?"

"Oh, no," I said loftily. "I'll give you five! You've got to try, anyway."

So she tried.

"In place of Revelation and Belief," she said slowly, "we now have Facts and Knowledge. We used to believe in God - variously, and teach the belief as a matter of duty. Now we know God, as much as we know anything else - more than we know anything else - it is The Fact of Life.

"This is the base of knowledge, underlying all other knowledge, simple and safe and sure - and we can teach it to children! The child mind, opening to this lovely world, is no longer filled with horrible or ridiculous old ideas - it learns to know the lovely truth of life."

She looked so serenely beautiful, and sat so still after she said this, that I felt a little awkward.

"I don't mean to jar on you, Nellie," I said. "I didn't know you were so - religious."

Then she laughed again merrily. "I'm not," she said. "No more than anybody is. We don't have 'religious' people any more, John. It's not a separate thing; a 'body of doctrine' and set of observances - it is what all of us have at the bottom of everything else, the underlying basic fact of life. And it goes far, very far indeed, to make the strong good cheer you see in these children's faces.

"They have never been frightened, John. They have never been told any of those awful things we used to tell them. There is no struggle with church-going, no gagging over doctrines, no mysterious queer mess - only life. Life is now open to our children, clear, brilliant, satisfying, and yet stimulating.

"Of course, I don't mean that this applies equally to every last one. The material benefit does, that could be enforced by law where necessary; but this world-wave of new knowledge is irregular, of course. It has spread wider, and gone faster than any of the old religions ever did, but you can find people yet who believe things almost as dreadful as father did!"

I well remembered my father's lingering Calvinism, and appreciated its horrors.

"Our educators have recognized a new duty to children," Nellie went on; "to stand between them and the past. We recognize that the child mind should lift and lead the world; and we feed it with our newest, not our oldest ideas.

"Also we encourage it to wander on ahead, fearless and happy. I began to tell you the other day - and you snubbed me, John, you did really! - that we have a new literature for children, and have dropped the old."

At this piece of information I could no longer preserve the attitude of a patient listener. I sat back and stared at my sister, while the full awfulness of this condition slowly rolled over me.

"Do you mean," I said slowly, "that children are taught nothing of the past?"

"Oh, no, indeed; they are taught about the past from the earth's beginning. In the mind of every child is a clear view of how Life has grown on earth."

"And our own history?"

"Of course; from savagery to today - that is a simple story, endlessly interesting as they grow older."

"What do you mean, then, by cutting off the past?"

"I mean that their stories, poems, pictures, and the major part of their instruction deals with the present and future - especially the future. The whole teaching is dynamic - not static. We used to teach mostly facts, or what we thought were facts. Now we teach processes. You'll find out if you talk to children, anywhere."

This I mentally determined to do, and in due course did. I may as well say right here that I found children more delightful companions than they used to be. They were polite enough, even considerate; but so universally happy, so overflowing with purposes, so skilful in so many ways, so intelligent and efficient, that it astonished me. We used to have a sort of race-myth about "happy childhood," but none of us seemed to study the faces of the children we saw about us. Even among well-to-do families, the discontented, careworn, anxious, repressed, or rebellious faces of children ought to have routed our myth forever.

Timid, brow-beaten children, sulky children, darkly resentful; nervous, whining children, foolish, mischievous, hysterically giggling children, noisy, destructive, uneasy children - how well I remembered them.

These new ones had a strange air of being Persons, not subordinates and dependents, but Equals; their limitations frankly admitted, but not cast up at them, and their special powers fully respected. That was it!

I am wandering far ahead of that day's conversation, but it led to wide study among children, analysis, and some interesting conclusions. When I hit on this one I began to understand. Children were universally respected, and they liked it. In city or country, place was made for them, permanent, pleasant, properly appointed place; to use, enjoy, and grow up in. They had their homes and families as before, losing nothing; but they added to this background their own wide gardens and houses, where part of each day was spent.

From earliest infancy they absorbed the idea that home was a place to come out from and go back to; the sweetest, dearest place - for there was mother, and father, and one's own little room to sleep in; but the day hours were to go somewhere to learn and do, to work and play, to grow in.

I branched off from Nellie's startling me with her "new-literature-for-children" idea. She went on to explain it further.

"The greatest artists work for children now, John," she said. "In the child-gardens and child-homes they are surrounded with beauty. I do not mean that we hire painters and poets to manufacture beauty for them; but that painters and poets, architects and landscape artists, designers and decorators of all kinds, love and revere childhood, and delight to work for it.

"Remember that half of our artists are mothers now - a loving, serving, giving spirit has come into expression - a wider and more lasting expression than it was ever possible to put into doughnuts and embroidery! Wait till you see the beauty of our child-gardens!"

"Why don't you call them schools? Don't you have schools?"

"Some. We haven't wholly outgrown the old academic habit. But for the babies there was no precedent, and they do not 'go to school.'"

"You have a sort of central nursery?" I ventured.

"Not necessarily 'central,' John. And we have great numbers of them. How can I make it any way clear to you? See here. Suppose you were a mother, and a very busy one, like the old woman in the shoe; and suppose you had twenty or thirty permanent babies to be provided for? And suppose you were wise and rich - able to do what you wanted to? Wouldn't you build an elaborate nursery for those children? Wouldn't you engage the very best nurses and teachers? Wouldn't you want the cleanest, quietest garden for them to play or sleep in? Of course you would.

"That is our attitude. We have at last recognized babies as a permanent class. They are always here, about a fifth of the population. And we, their mothers, have at last ensured to these, our babies, the best accommodation known to our time. It improves as we learn, of course."

"Mm!" I said. "I'll go and gaze upon these Infant Paradises later - at the sleeping hour, please! But how about that new literature you frightened me with?"

"Oh. Why, we have tried to treat their minds as we do their stomachs - putting in only what is good for then. I mean the very littlest, understand. As they grow older they have wider range; we have not expunged the world's past, my dear brother! But we do prepare with all the wisdom, love, and power we have, the mental food for little children. Simple, lovely music is about them always - you must have noticed how universally they sing?"

I had, and said so.

"The coloring and decoration of their rooms is beautiful - their clothes are beautiful - and simple - you've seen that, too?"

"Yes, dear girl. It's because I've seen - and heard - and noticed the surprisingness of the New Child that I sit here fairly guzzling information. Pray proceed to the literature."

"Literature is the most useful of the arts - the most perfect medium for transfer of ideas. We wish to have the first impressions in our children's minds, above all things, true. All the witchery and loveliness possible in presentation - but the things presented are not senseless and unpleasant.

"We have plenty of 'true stories,' stories based on real events and on natural laws and processes; but the viewpoint from which they are written has changed; you'll have to read some to see what I mean. But the major difference is in our stories of the future, our future here on earth. They are good stories, mind, the very best writers make them; good verses and pictures, too. And a diet like that, while it is just as varied and entertaining as the 'once upon a time' kind, leaves the child with a sense that things are going to happen - and he, or she, can help.

"You see, we don't consider anything as done. To you, as a new visitor, we 'point with pride,' but among ourselves we 'view with alarm.' We are just as full of Reformers and Propagandists as ever, and overflowing with plans for improvement.

"These are the main characteristics of the new child literature: Truth and Something Better Ahead."

"I don't like it!" I said firmly. "No wonder you dodged about so long. You've apparently made a sort of pap out of Grad-grind and Rollo, and feed it to these poor babies through a tube."

This time my sister rebelled. She came firmly to my side and pulled my hair - precisely as she used to do forty years ago and more - the few little hairs at the crown which still troubled me in brushing - because of being pulled out straight so often.

"You shall have no more oral instruction, young man," said she. "You shall be taken about and shown things; you shall 'Stop! Look! Listen!' until you admit the advantages I have striven in vain to pump into your resisting intellect - you Product of Past Methods!"

"You're the product of the same methods yourself, my dear," I replied amiably; "but I'm quite willing to be shown - always was something of a Missourian."

No part of my re-education was pleasanter, and I'm sure none was more important, than the next few days. We visited place after place, in different cities, or in the country, and everywhere was the same high standard of health and beauty, of comfort, fun, and visible growth.

I saw babies and wee toddlers by the thousands, and hardly ever heard one cry! Out of that mass of experience some vivid pictures remain in my mind. One was "mother time" in a manufacturing village. There was a big group of mills with water-power; each mill a beautiful, clean place, light, airy, rich in color, sweet with the flowers about it, where men and women worked their two-hour shifts.

The women took off their work-aprons and slipped into the neighboring garden to nurse their babies. They were in no haste. They were pleasantly dressed and well-fed and not tired.

They were known and welcomed by the women in charge of the child-garden; and each mother slipped into a comfortable rocker and took into her arms that little rosy piece of herself and the man she loved - it was a thing to bring one's heart into one's throat. The clean peace and quiet of it, time enough, the pleasant neighborliness, the atmosphere of contented motherhood, those healthy, drowsy little mites, so busy with their dinner.

Then they put them down, asleep. For the most part, kissed them, and strolled back to the pleasant workroom for another two hours.

Specialization used to be a terror, when a whole human being was held down to one notion for ten hours. But specialization hurts nobody when it does not last too long.

In the afternoons some mothers took their babies home at once. Some nursed them and then went out together for exercise or pleasure. The homes were clean and quiet, too; no kitchen work, no laundry work, no self-made clutter and dirt. It looked so comfortable that I couldn't believe my eyes, yet it was just common, everyday life.

As the babies grew old enough to move about, their joys widened. They were kept in rooms of a suitable temperature, and wore practically no clothes. This in itself I was told was one main cause of their health and contentment. They rolled and tumbled on smooth mattresses; pulled themselves up and swung back and forth on large, soft horizontal ropes fastened within reach; delightful little bunches of rose leaves and dimples, in perfect happiness.

Very early they had water to play in; clean, shallow pools, kept at a proper temperature, where they splashed and gurgled in rapture, and learned to swim before they learned to walk, sometimes.

As they grew larger and more competent, their playgrounds were more extensive and varied; but the underlying idea was always clear - safety and pleasure, full exercise and development of every power. There was no quarrelling over toys - whatever they had to play with they all had in abundance; and most of the time they did not have exchangeable objects, but these ropes, pools, sand, clay, and so on, materials common to all; and the main joy was in the use of their own little bodies, is as many ways as was possible.

At any time when they were not asleep a procession of crowing toddlers could be seen creeping up a slight incline and sliding or rolling triumphantly down the other side. A sort of beautified cellar door, this.

Strange that we always punished children for sliding down unsuitable things and never provided suitable ones. But then, of course, one could not have machinery like this in one brief family. Swings, see-saws, all manner of moving things they had, with building-blocks, of course, and balls. But as soon as it was easy to them they had tools and learned to use them; the major joy of their expanding lives was doing things. I speak of them in an unbroken line, for that was the way they lived. Each stage lapped over into the next, and that natural ambition to be with the older ones and do what they did was the main incentive in their progress.

To go on, to get farther, higher, to do something better and more interesting, this was in the atmosphere; growth, exercise, and joy.

I watched and studied, and grew happy as I did so; which I could see was a gratification to Nellie.

"Aren't they ever naughty?" I demanded one day.

"Why should they be?" she answered. "How could they be? What we used to call 'naughtiness' was only the misfit. The poor little things were in the wrong place - and nobody knew how to make them happy. Here there is nothing they can hurt, and nothing that can hurt them. They have earth, air, fire, and water to play with."

"Fire?" I interrupted.

"Yes, indeed. All children love fire, of course. As soon as they can move about they are taught fire."

"How many burn themselves up?"

"None. Never any more. Did you never hear 'a burnt child dreads the fire'? We said that, but we never had sense enough to use it. No proverb ever said 'a whipped child dreads the fire'! We never safe-guarded them, and the poor little things were always getting burned to death in our barbarous 'homes'!"

"Do you arbitrarily burn them all?" I asked. "Have an annual 'branding'?"

"Oh, no; but we allow them to burn themselves - within reason. Come and see."

She showed me a set of youngsters learning Heat and Cold, with basins of water, a row of them; eagerly experimenting with cautious little fingers - very cold, cold, cool, tepid, warm, hot, very hot. They could hardly say the words plain, but learned them all, even when they all had to shut their eyes and the basins were changed about.

Straying from house to house, from garden to garden, I watched them grow and learn. On the long walls about them were painted an endless panorama of human progress. When they noticed and asked questions they were told, without emphasis, that people used to live that way; and grew to this - and this.

I found that as the children grew older they all had a year of travel; each human being knew his world. And when I questioned as to expense, as I always did, Nellie would flatten me with things like this:

"Remember that we used to spend 70 per cent, of our national income on the expenses of war, past and present. If we women had done no more than save that, it would have paid for all you see."

Or she would remind me again of the immense sums we used to spend on hospitals and prisons; or refer to the general change in economics, that inevitable socialization of industry, which had checked waste and increased productivity so much.

"We are a rich people, John," she repeated. "So are other nations, for that matter; the world's richer. We have increased our output and lowered our expenses at the same time. One of our big present problems is what to do with our big surplus; we quarrel roundly over that. But meanwhile it is a very poor nation indeed that does not provide full education for its children."

I found that the differences in education were both subtle and profound. The babies' experience of group life, as well as the daily return to family life, gave a sure ground-work for the understanding of civics. Their first impressions included other babies; no child grew up with the intensified self-consciousness we used to almost force upon them.

In all the early years learning was ceaseless and unconscious. They grew among such carefully chosen surroundings as made it impossible not to learn what was really necessary; and to learn it as squirrels learn the trees - by playing and working in them. They learned the simple beginnings of the world's great trades, led by natural interest and desire, gathering by imitation and asked instruction.

I saw nowhere the enforced task; everywhere the eager attention of real interest.

"Are they never taught to apply themselves? To concentrate?" I asked. And for answer she showed me the absorbed, breathless concentration of fresh young minds and busy hands.

"But they soon tire of these things and want to do something else, do they not?"

"Of course. That is natural to childhood. And there is always something else for them to do."

"But they are only doing what they like to do - that is no preparation for a life work surely."

"We find it an excellent preparation for life work. You see, we all work at what we like now. That is one reason we do so much better work."

I had talked on this line before with those who explained the workings of industrial socialism.

"Still, as a matter of education," I urged, "is it not necessary for a child to learn to compel himself to work?"

"Oh, no," they told me; and, to say truth, convincingly showed me. "Children like to work. If any one does not, we know he is sick."

And as I saw more and more of the child-gardens, and sat silently watching for well-spent hours, I found how true this was.

The children had around them the carefully planned stimuli of a genuinely educational environment. The work of the world was there, in words of one syllable, as it were; and among wise, courteous, pleasant people, themselves actually doing something, yet always ready to give information when asked.

First the natural appetite of the young brain, then every imaginable convenience for learning, then the cautiously used accessories to encourage further effort; and then these marvelous teachers - who seemed to like their work, too. The majority were women, and of them nearly all were mothers. It appeared that children had not lost their mothers, as at first one assumed, but that each child kept his own and gained others. And these teaching mothers were somehow more motherly than the average.

Nellie was so pleased when I noticed this. She liked to see me "going to school" so regularly. I was not alone in it, either. There seemed to be numbers of people who cared enough for children to enjoy watching them and playing with them. Nobody was worn out with child care. The parents were not - the nurses and teachers had short shifts - it seemed to be considered a pleasure and an honor to be allowed with the little ones.

And in all this widespread, costly, elaborate, and yet perfectly simple and lovely environment, these little New Persons grew and blossomed with that divine unconsciousness which belongs to children.

They did not know that the best intellects were devoted to their service, they never dreamed what thought and love and labor made these wide gardens, these bright playing-places, these endlessly interesting shops where they could learn to make things as soon as they were old enough. They took it all as life - just Life, as a child must take his first environment.

"And don't you think, John," Nellie said, when I spoke of this, "don't you really think this is a more normal environment for a young human soul than a kitchen? Or a parlor? Or even a nursery?"

I had to admit that it had its advantages. As they grew older there was every chance for specialization. In the first years they gathered the rudiments of general knowledge, and of general activity, of both hand and brain, and from infancy each child was studied, and his growth - or hers - carefully recorded; not by adoring, intimately related love, but by that larger, wiser tenderness of these great child-lovers who had had hundreds of them to study.

They were observed intelligently. Notes were made, the mother and father contributed theirs; in freedom and unconscious-ness the young nature developed, never realizing how its environment was altered to fit its special needs.

As the cool, spacious, flower-starred, fruitful forests of this time differed from the tangled underbrush, with crooked, crowded, imperfect trees struggling for growth, that I remembered as "woods," or from clipped and twisted products of the forcing and pruning process; so did the new child-gardens differ from the old schools.

No wonder children wore so different an aspect. They had the fresh, insatiable thirst for knowledge which has been wisely slaked, but never given the water-torture. As I recalled my own youth, and thought of all those young minds set in rows, fixed open as with a stick between the teeth, and forced to drink, drink, drink till all desire was turned to loathing, I felt a sudden wish to be born again - now! - and begin over.

As an adult observer, I found this re-arranged world jarring and displeasing in many ways; but as I sat among the children, played with them, talked with them, became somewhat acquainted with their views of things, I began to see that to them the new world was both natural and pleasant.

When they learned that I was a "left-over" from what to them seemed past ages, I became extremely popular. There was a rush to get near me, and eager requests to tell them about old times - checked somewhat by politeness, yet always eager.

But the cheerful pride with which I began to describe the world as I knew it was considerably dashed by their comments. What I had considered as necessary evils, or as no evils at all, to them appeared as silly and disgraceful as cannibalism; and there grew among them an attitude of chivalrous pity for my unfortunate upbringing which was pretty to see.

"I see no child in glasses!" I suddenly remarked one day.

"Of course not," answered the teacher I stood by. "We use books very little, you see. Education no longer impairs our machinery."

I recalled the Boston school children and the myopic victims of Germany's archaic letter-press; and freely admitted that this was advance. Much of the instruction was oral - much, very much, came through games and exercises; books, I found, were regarded rather as things to consult, like a dictionary, or as instruments of high enjoyment.

"School books" - "text books" - scarcely existed, at least for children. The older ones, some of them, plunged into study with passion; but their eyes were good and their brains were strong; also their general health. There was no "breakdown from overstudy;" that slow, cruel, crippling injury - sometimes death, which we, wise and loving parents of past days, so frequently forced upon our helpless children.

Naturally happy, busy, self-respecting, these grew up; with a wide capacity for action, a breadth of general knowledge which was almost incredible, a high standard of courtesy, and vigorous, well-exercised minds. They were trained to think, I found; to question, discuss, decide; they could reason.

And they faced life with such loving enthusiasm! Such pride in the new accomplishments of the world! Such a noble, boundless ambition to do things, to make things, to help the world still further.

And from infancy to adolescence - all through these years of happy growing - there was nothing whatever to differentiate the boys from the girls! As a rule, they could not be distinguished.

CHAPTER 10

It was this new growth of humanity which made continuing social progress so rapid and so sure.

These young minds had no rubbish in them. They had a vivid sense of the world as a whole, quite beyond their family "relations." They were marvelously reasonable, free from prejudice, able to see and willing to do. And this spreading tide of hope and courage flowed back into the older minds, as well as forward into the new.

I found that people's ideas of youth and age had altered materially. Nellie said it was due to the change in women - but then she laid most things to that. She reminded me that women used to be considered only as females, and were "old" when no longer available in that capacity; but that as soon as they recognized themselves as human beings they put "Grandma" into the background, and "Mother" too; and simply went on working and growing and enjoying life up into the lively eighties - even nineties, sometimes.

"Brains do not cease to function at fifty," she said. "Just because a woman is no longer an object to 'fall in love' with, it does not follow that life has no charms for her. Women today have all that they ever had before, all that was good in it; and more, a thousand times more. When the lives of half the world widen like that it widens the other half too."

This quite evidently had happened.

The average mental standard was higher, the outlook broader. I found many very ordinary people, of course; some whose only attitude toward this wonderful new world was to enjoy its advantages; and even some who grumbled. These were either old persons with bad digestions or new immigrants from very backward countries.

I traveled about, visiting different places, consulting all manner of authorities, making notes, registering objections. It was all interesting, and grew more so as it seemed less strange. My sense of theatrical unreality gave way to a growing appreciation of the universal beauty about me.

Art, I found, held a very different position from what it used to hold. It had joined hands with life again, was common, familiar, used in all things. There were pictures, many and beautiful, but the great word Art was no longer so closely confined to its pictorial form. It was not narrow, expensive, requiring a special education, but part of the atmosphere in which all children grew, all people lived.

For instance the theatre, which I remember as a two-dollar affair, and mainly vulgar and narrow, was now the daily companion and teacher. The historic instinct with which nearly every child is born was cultivated without check. The little ones played through all their first years of instruction, played the old stone age (most natural to them!) the new stone age, the first stages of industry. Older children learned history that way; and as they reached years of appreciation, special dramas were written for them, in which psychology and sociology were learned without hearing their names.

Those happy, busy, eager young things played gaily through wide ranges of human experience; and when these emotions touched them in later years, they were not strange and awful, but easy to understand.

In every smallest village there was a playhouse, not only in the child-gardens, but for the older people. They each had their dramatic company, as some used to have their bands; had their musical companies too, and better ones.

Out of this universal use of the drama rose freely those of special talent who made it the major business of their lives; and the higher average everywhere gave to these greater ones the atmosphere of real appreciation which a growing art must have.

I asked Nellie how the people managed who lived in the real country - remote and alone.

"We don't live that way any more," she said. "Only some stubborn old people, like Uncle Jake and Aunt Dorcas. You see the women decided that they must live in groups to have proper industrial and educational advantages; and they do."

"Where do the men live?" I asked grimly.

"With the women, of course - Where should they? I don't mean that a person cannot go and live in a hut on a mountain, if he likes; we do that in summer, very largely. It is a rest to be alone part of the time. But living, real human living, requires a larger group than one family. You can see the results."

I could and I did; though I would not always admit it to Nellie; and this beautiful commonness of good music, good architecture, good sculpture, good painting, good drama, good dancing, good literature, impressed me increasingly. Instead of those perpendicular peaks of isolated genius we used to have, surrounded by the ignorantly indifferent many, and the excessively admiring few, those geniuses now sloped gently down to the average on long graduated lines of decreasing ability. It gave to the commonest people a possible road of upward development, and to the most developed a path of connection with the commonest people. The geniuses seemed to like it too. They were not so conceited, not so disagreeable, not so lonesome.

People seemed to have a very good time, even while at work; indeed very many found their work more fun than anything else. The abundant leisure gave a sort of margin to life which was wholly new, to the majority at least. It was that spare time, and the direct efforts of the government in wholesale educational lines, which had accomplished so much in the first ten years.

Owen reminded me of the educational vitality even of the years I knew; of the university extension movement, the lectures in the public schools, the push of the popular magazines; the summer schools, the hundreds of thousands of club women, whose main effort seemed to be to improve their minds.

"And the Press," I said - "our splendid Press."

"That was one of our worst obstacles, I'm sorry to say," he answered.

I looked at him. "Oh, go ahead, go ahead! You'll tell me the public schools were an obstacle next."

"They would have been - if we hadn't changed them," he agreed. "But they were in our hands at least, and we got them re-arranged very promptly. That absurd old despotism which kept the grade of teachers down so low, was very promptly changed. We have about five times as many teachers now, fifty times as good and far better paid, not only in cash, but in public appreciation. Our teachers are 'leading citizens' now - we have elected one President from the School Principalship of a state."

This was news, and not unpleasant.

"Have you elected any Editors?"

"No - but we may soon. They are a new set of men now I can tell you; and women, of course. You remember in our day journalism was frankly treated as a trade; whereas it is visibly one of the most important professions."

"And did you so reform those Editors, so that they became as self-sacrificing as country doctors?"

"Oh, no. But we changed the business conditions. It was the advertising that corrupted the papers - mostly; and the advertisers were only screaming for bread and butter - especially butter. When Socialism reorganized business there was no need to scream."

"But I find plenty of advertising in the papers and magazines."

"Certainly - it is a great convenience. Have you studied it?"

I had to own that I had not particularly - I never did like advertising.

"You'll find it worth reading. In the first place it's all true."

"How do you secure that?"

"We have made lying to the public a crime - don't you remember? Each community has its Board of Standards; there is a constant effort to improve standards you see, in all products; and expert judgment may always be had, for nothing. If any salesman advertises falsely he loses his job, if he's an official; and is posted, if he's selling as a private individual. When the public is told officially that Mr. Jones is a liar it hurts his trade."

"You have a Government Press?"

"Exactly. The Press is preeminently a public function - it is not and never was a private business - not legitimately."

"But you do have private papers and magazines?"

"Yes indeed, lots of them. Ever so many personal 'organs' large and small. But they don't carry advertising. If enough people will buy a man's paper to pay him, he's quite free to publish."

"How do you prevent his carrying advertising?"

"It's against the law - like any other misdemeanor. Post Office won't take it - he can't distribute. No, if you want to find out about the latest breakfast food - (and there are a score you never heard of) - or the last improvement in fountain pens or air-ships - you find it all, clear, short, and reliable, in the hotel paper of every town. There's no such bulk of advertising matter now, you see; not so many people struggling to sell the same thing."

"Is all business socialized?"

"Yes - and no. All the main business is; the big assured steady things that our life depends on. But there is a free margin for individual initiative - and always will be. We are not so foolish as to cut off that supply. We have more inventors and idealists than ever; and plenty of chance for trial. You see the two hours a day which pays board, so to speak, leaves plenty of time to do other work; and if the new thing the man does is sufficiently valuable to enough people, he is free to do that alone. Like the little one-man papers I spoke of. If a man can find five thousand people who will pay a dollar a year to read what he says he's quite as likely to make his living that way."

"Have you no competition at all?"

"Plenty of it. All our young folks are? racing and chasing to break the record; to do more work, better work, new work."

"But not under the spur of necessity."

"Why, yes they are. The most compelling necessity we know. They *have* to do it; it is in them and must come out."

"But they are all sure of a living, aren't they?"

"Yes, of course. Oh, I see! What you meant by necessity was hunger and cold. Bless you, John, poverty was no spur. It was a deadly anaesthetic."

I looked my disagreement, and he went on: "You remember the hideous poverty and helplessness of the old days - did that 'spur' the population to do anything? Don't you see, John, that if poverty had been the splendid stimulus it used to be thought, there wouldn't have been any poverty? Some few exceptional persons triumphed in spite of it, but we shall never know the amount of world loss in the many who did not.

"It was funny," he continued meditatively, "how we went on believing that in some mysterious way poverty 'strengthened character,' 'developed initiative,' 'stimulated industry,' and did all manner of fine things; and never turned our eyes on the millions of people who lived and died in poverty with weakened characters, no initiative, a slow, enforced and hated industry. My word, John, what fools we were!"

I was considering this Government Press he described. "How did you dispose of the newspapers you had?"

"Just as we disposed of the saloons; drove them out of business by underselling them with better goods. The laws against lying helped too."

"I don't see how you can stop people's lying"

"We can't stop their lying in private, except by better social standards; but we can stop public lying, and we have. If a paper published a false statement anyone could bring a complaint; and the district attorney was obliged to prosecute. If a paper pleaded ignorance or misinformation it was let off with a fine and a reprimand the first time, a heavy fine the second time, and confiscation the third time; as being proved by their own admission incompetent to tell the truth! If it was shown to be an intentional falsehood they were put out of business at once."

"That's all very pretty," I said, "and sounds easy as you tell it; but what made people so hot about lying? They didn't used to mind it. The more you tell me of these things the more puzzled I am as to what altered the minds of the people. They certainly had to alter considerably from the kind I remember, to even want all these changes, much more to enforce them."

Owen wasn't much of a psychologist, and said so. He insisted that people had wanted better things, only they did not know it.

"Well - what made them know it?" I insisted. "Now here's one thing, small in a way, but showing a very long step in alteration; people dress comfortably and beautifully; almost all of them. What made them do it?"

"They have more money," Owen began, "more leisure and better education."

But I waved this aside.

"That has nothing to do with it. The people with money and education were precisely the ones who wore the most outrageous clothes. And as to leisure - they spent their leisure in getting up foolish costumes, apparently."

"Women are more intelligent, you see," he began again; but I dismissed this also.

"The intelligence of a Lord Chancellor didn't prevent his wearing a wig! How did people break loose from the force of fashion, I want to know?"

He could not make this clear, and said he wouldn't try.

"You show me all these material changes," I went on; "and I can see that there was no real obstacle to them; but the obstacle that lasted so long was in the people's minds. What moved that? Then you show me this marvellous new education, as resulting in new kinds of people, better people, wiser, freer, stronger, braver; and I can see that at work. But how did you come to accept this new education? You needn't lay it all to the women, as Nellie does. I knew one or two of the most advanced of them in 1910, and they had no such world-view as this. They wore foolish clothes and had no ideas beyond 'Votes for Women' - some of them."

"No sir! I admit that there was potential wealth enough in the earth to support all this ease and beauty; and potential energy in the people to produce the wealth. I admit that it was possible for people to leave off being stupid and become wise - evidently they have done so. But I don't see what made them."

"You go and see Dr. Borderson," said Owen.

CHAPTER 11

Dr.Borderson, it seemed, held the chair in Ethics at the University, I knew a Borderson once and was very fond of him. Poor Frank! If he was alive he would have more likely reached a prison or a hospital than a professorship. Yet he was brilliant enough. We were great friends in college, and before; let me see - thirty-five years ago. But he was expelled for improper conduct, and went from bad to worse. The last I had heard of him was in a criminal case - but he had run away and disappeared. I well remembered the grief and shame it was to me at the time to see such a promising young life ruined and lost so early.

Thinking of this, I was shown into the study of the great teacher of ethics, and as I shook hands I met the keen brown eyes of - Frank Borderson. He had both my hands and shook them warmly.

"Well, John! It is good to see you again. How well you look; how little you have changed! It's a good world you've come back to, isn't it?"

"You are the most astonishing thing I've seen so far," I replied. "Do you really mean it? Are you - a Professor of Ethics?"

"When I used to be a God-forsaken rascal, eh? Yes, it's really so. I've taught Ethics for twenty years, and gradually pushed along to this position. And I was a good deal farther off than Tibet, old man."

I was tremendously glad to see him. It was more like a touch of the old life than anything I had yet found - except Nellie, of course. We spoke for some time of those years of boyhood; of the good times we had had together; of our common friends.

He kept me to dinner; introduced me to his wife, a woman with a rather sad, sweet face, which seemed to bear marks of deep experience; and we settled down for an evening's talk.

"I think you have come to the right person, John; not only because of my special studies, but because of my special line of growth. If I can tell you what changed me, so quickly and so wholly, you won't be much puzzled about the others, eh?"

I fully agreed with him. The boy I knew was clever enough to dismiss all theology, to juggle with philosophy and pick ethics to pieces; but his best friends had been reluctantly compelled to admit that he had "no moral character." He had, to my knowledge, committed a number of unquestionable "sins," and by hearsay I knew of vices and crimes that followed. And he was Dr. Borderson!

"I'll take myself as a sample, Whitman fashion," said he. "There I was when you knew me - conceited, ignorant, clever, self-indulgent, weak, sensual, dishonest. After I was turned out of college I broke a good many laws and nearly all the commandments. What was worse, in one way, was that my 'wages' were being paid me in disease - abominable disease. Also I had two drug habits - alchohol and cocaine. Will you take me as a sample?"

I looked at him. He had not the perfect health I saw so much of in the younger people; but he seemed in no way an invalid, much less a drug victim. His eyes were clear and bright, his complexion good, his hand steady, his manner assured and calm.

"Frank," said I, "you beat anything I've seen yet. You stand absolutely to my mind as an illustration of 'Before Taking' and 'After Taking.' Now in the name of reason tell me what it was you Took!"

"I took a new grip on Life - that's the whole answer. But you want to know the steps, and I'll tell you. The new stage of ethical perception we are in now - or, as you would probably say, this new religion - presents itself to me in this way:

"The business of the universe about us consists in the Transmission of Energy. Some of it is temporarily and partially arrested in material compositions; some is more actively expressed in vegetable and animal form; this stage of expression we call Life. We ourselves, the human animals, were specially adapted for high efficiency in storing and transmitting this energy; and so were able to enter into a combination still more efficient; that is, into social relations. Humanity, man in social relation, is the best expression of the Energy that we know. This Energy is what the human mind has been conscious of ever since it was conscious at all; and calls God. The relation between this God and this Humanity is in reality a very simple one. In common with all other life forms, the human being must express itself in normal functioning. Because of its special faculty of consciousness, this human engine can feel, see, think, about the power within it; and can use it more fully and wisely. All it has to learn is the right expression of its degree of life-force, of Social Energy." He beamed at me. "I think it's about all there, John."

"You may be a very good Professor of Ethics for these new-made minds, but you don't reach the old kind - not a little bit. To my mind you haven't said anything - yet."

He seemed a little disappointed, but took it mildly. "Perhaps I am a little out of touch. Wait a moment - let me go back and try to take up the old attitude."

He leaned back in his chair and shut his eyes, I saw an expression of pain slowly grow and deepen on his face; and suddenly realized what he was doing.

"Oh, never mind, Frank; don't do it; don't try, I'll catch on somehow."

He seemed not to hear me; but dropped his face in his hands. When he raised it it was clear again. "Now I can make things clearer perhaps," he said. "We had in our minds thirty years ago a strange hodge-podge of old and new ideas. What was called God was still largely patterned after the old tribal deity of the Hebrews. Our ideas of 'Sin' were still mostly of the nature of disobedience -

wrong only because we were told not to do it. Sin as a personal offence against Somebody, and Somebody very much offended; that was it. We were beginning to see something of Social values, too, but not clearly. Our progress was in what we called 'The natural sciences'; and we did not think with the part of our minds wherein we stored religion. Yet there was very great activity and progress in religious thought; the whole field was in motion; the new churches widening and growing in every direction; the older ones holding on like grim death, trying not to change, and changing in spite of themselves; and Ethics being taught indeed, but with no satisfying basis. That's the kind of atmosphere you and I grew up in, John. Now here was I, an ill-assorted team of impulses and characteristics, prejudiced against religion, ignorant of real ethics, and generally going to the devil - as we used to call it! You know how far down I went - or something of it."

"Don't speak of it, Frank!" I said. "That was long ago; forget it, old man!" But he turned toward me a smile of triumph.

"Forget it! I wouldn't forget one step of it if I could! Why, John, it's because of my intimate knowledge of these down-going steps that I can help people up them!"

"You looked decidedly miserable just now, all the same, when you were thinking them over."

"Oh, bless you, John, I wasn't thinking of myself at all! I was thinking of the awful state of mind the world was in, and how it suffered! Of all the horror and misery and shame; all that misplaced, unnecessary cruelty we called punishment; the Dark Ages we were still in, in spite of all we had to boast of. However, this new perception came."

I interrupted him.

"What came? Who came? Did you have a new revelation? Who did it? What do you call it? Nobody seems to be able to give me definite information."

He smiled broadly. "You're a beautiful proof of the kind of mental jumble I spoke of. Knowledge of evolution did not come by a revelation, did it? Or did any one man, or two, give it to us? Darwin and Wallace were not the only minds that helped to see and express that great idea; and many more had to spread it. These great truths break into the world-mind through various individuals, and coalesce so that we cannot disconnect them. We have had many writers, preachers, lecturers, who discoursed and explained; this new precept as to the relation between man and God came with such a general sweep that no one even tries to give personal credit for it. These things are not personal - they are world-percepts."

"But every religion has had its Founder, hasn't it?"

"We don't call it a religion, my dear fellow! It's a science, like any other science. Ethics is The Science of Human Relation. It is called Applied Sociology - that's all."

"How does a thing like that touch one, personally?" I asked.

"How does any science touch one personally? One studies a science, one teaches a science, one uses a science. That's the point - the use of it. Our old scheme of religion was a thing to 'believe,' or 'deny'; it was a sort of shibboleth, a test question one had to pass examination in to get good marks! What I'm telling you about is a general recognition of right behavior, and a general grasp of the necessary power."

"You leave out entirely the emotional side of religion."

"Do I? I did not intend to. You see, we do not distinguish religion from life now, and are apt to forget old terms. You are thinking, I suppose, of the love of God, and man, which we used to preach. We practice it now.

"That Energy I spoke of, when perceived by us, is called Love. Love, the real thing we had in mind when we said 'God is Love,' is beneficent energy. It is the impulse of service, the desire to do, to help, to make, to benefit. That is the 'love' we were told to bestow on one another. Now we do."

"Yes; but what made you do it? What keeps you up to it?"

"Just nature, John. It is human nature. We used to believe otherwise." He was quiet for a while.

"One of these new doctors got hold of me, when I was about as near the bottom as one can go and get back. Not a priest with a formula, nor a reformer with an exhortation; but a real physician, a soul-doctor, with a passionate enthusiasm for an interesting case. That's what I was, John; not a lost soul; not even a 'sinner' - just 'a case.' Have you heard about these moral sanitariums?"

"Yes - but not definitely."

"Well, as soon as this view of things took hold, they began to want to isolate bad cases, and cure them if they could. And they cured me."

"How, Frank - how? What did they tell you that you didn't know before? What did they do to you?"

"Sane, strong, intelligent minds put themselves in connection with mine, John, and shared their strength with me. I was made to feel that my individual failure was no great matter, but that my social duty was; that the whole of my dirty past was as nothing to all our splendid future, that whatever I had done was merely to be forgotten - the sooner the better, and that all life was open before me - all human life; endless, beautiful, profoundly interesting - the game was on, and I was in it.

"John - I wish I could make you feel it. It was as if we had all along had inside us an enormous reservoir of love, human love, that had somehow been held in and soured! This new arrangement of our minds let it out - to our limitless relief and joy. No 'sin' - think of that! Just let it sink in. No such thing as sin... We had, collectively and privately, made mistakes, and done the wrong thing, often. What of it? Of course we had. A growing race *grew that way.*

"Now we are wiser and need not keep on going wrong. We had learned that life was far easier, pleasanter, more richly satisfying when followed on these new lines - and the new lines were not hard to learn. Love was the natural element of social life. Love meant service, service meant doing one's special work well, and doing it for the persons served - of course!

"*All* our mistakes lay in our belated Individualism. You cannot predicate Ethics of individuals; you cannot fulfill any religion as individuals. My fellow creatures took hold of me, you see. That power that was being used so extensively for physical healing in our young days had become a matter of common knowledge - and use."

"How many of these - moral hygienists - did you have?"

"Scores, hundreds, thousands - we all help one another now. If a person is tired and blue and has lost his grip, if he can't rectify it by change of diet and change of scene, he goes to a moral hygienist, as you rightly call it, and gets help. I do a lot of that sort of work."

I meditated awhile, and again shook my head. "I'm afraid it's no use. I can't make it seem credible. I hear what you say and I see what you've done - but I do not get any clear understanding of the process. With people as they were, with all those case-hardened old sinners, all the crass ignorance, the stupidity, the sodden prejudice, the apathy, the selfishness - to make a world like that see reason - in thirty years! - No - I don't get it."

"You are wrong in your premises, John. Human nature is, and was, just as good as the rest of nature. Two things kept us back - wrong conditions, and wrong ideas; we have changed both. I think you forget the sweeping advance in material conditions and its effect on character. What made the well-bred, well-educated, well-meaning, pleasant people we used to know? Good conditions, for them and their ancestors. There were just as pleasant people among the poor and among their millions of children; they had every capacity for noble growth - given the chance. It took no wholesale change of heart to make people want shorter hours, better pay, better housing, food, clothes, amusements. As soon as the shameful pressure of poverty was taken off humanity it rose like a freed spring. Humanity's all right."

"There were some things all wrong," I replied, "that I know. You could not obliterate hereditary disease in ten - or thirty years. You couldn't make clean women of hundreds of thousands of prostitutes. You couldn't turn an invalid tramp into a healthy gentleman."

He stopped me. "We could do better than that," he said, "and we have. I begin to see your central difficulty, John; the difficulty that used to hold us all. You are looking at life as a personal affair - a matter of personal despair or salvation."

"Of course, what else is it?"

"What *else*! Why, that is no part of human life! Human life is social, John, collectively, common, or it isn't human life at all. Hereditary disease looks pretty hopeless when you see one generation or two or three so cursed. But when you realize how swiftly the stream of human life can be cleansed of it, you take a fresh hold. The percentage of hereditary disease has sunk by more than half in thirty years, John, and at its present rate of decrease will be gone, clean gone, in another twenty. Remember that every case is known, and that they are either prevented from transmitting the inheritance, isolated, or voluntarily living single. Diseases from bad conditions we no longer endure, nor diseases from ignorance, those from *bacilli* we are able to resist or cure; disease was never a permanent thing - only an accident. As for the prostitutes - we thought them 'ruined' because they were no longer suitable for our demands in marriage. As if that was everything! I tell you we opened a way out for them!"

"Namely?"

"Namely all the rest of life! Sex-life isn't everything, John. Not fit to be a mother, we said to them; never mind - there is everything else in the world to be. You may remember, my friend, that thousands of men, as vicious as any prostitutes, and often as diseased, continued to live, to work, and to enjoy. Why shouldn't the women? You haven't ruined your lives, we said to them; only one part. It's a loss, a great loss, but never mind, the whole range of human life remains open to you, the great moving world of service and growth and happiness. If you're sick, you're sick - we'll cure it if possible. If not, you'll die - never mind, we all die - that's nothing."

"Does your new religion call death nothing?"

"Certainly. The fuss we made about death was wholly owing to the old religions; the post-mortem religions, their whole basis was death."

"Hold on a bit. Do you mean to tell me the people aren't afraid of death any more?"

"Not a bit. Why should they be? Every living thing dies; that's part of the living. We do not hide it from children now, we teach it to them."

"Teach death - to children! How horrible!"

"Did you see or hear anything horrible in your educational excursions, John? I know you didn't. No, they learn it naturally; in their gardens; in their autumn and winter songs; in their familiarity with insects and animals. Our children learn life, death, and immortality, from silk-worms; and, then only incidentally. The silk is what they are studying.

"It takes a great many silk-worms to make silk, generations of them. They see them born, live and die, as incidents in silk culture. So we show them how people are born, live and die, in the making of human history. The idea is worked into our new educational literature - and all our literature for that matter. We see human life as a continuous whole now. People are only temporary parts of it. Dying isn't any more trouble than being born.

"People feared death, originally, because it hurt; being chased and eaten was not pleasant. But natural dying does not hurt. Then they were made to fear it by the hell-school of religions. All that is gone by. Our religion rests on life."

"The life of this world or the life eternal?"

"The eternal life of this world, John. We have no quarrel with anyone's belief as to what may happen after death, that is a free field; but the glory and power of our religion is that it rests with assurance on common knowledge of the beautiful facts of life. Here is Humanity, a continuing stream of life. Its line of advance is clear. That which makes Humanity stronger, wiser and happier is evidently what is right for it to do. We do teach it to all our children."

"And they do it?"

"Of course they do it. Why shouldn't they?"

"But our evil tendencies "

"We don't have evil tendencies, John - and never did. We have earlier and later tendencies; and it is perfectly possible to show the child which is which."

"But surely it is easier to follow the lower impulses than the higher; easier to give way than to strive."

"There's the old misconception, John, that Striving idea. We assumed that it was 'natural' to be 'bad' and 'unnatural' to be 'good' - that we had to make special efforts, painful and laborious, to become better. We had not seen, thirty years ago, that social evolution is as 'natural' as the evolution of the horse from the *eohippus*. If it was easier to be an *eohippus* than a horse why did the thing change?

"As to that army of 'fallen women' you are so anxious about, they just got up again, that's all, got up and went on. They had only fallen from one position; there was plenty of room left to stand and walk. Why they were not a speck on society compared to the 'fallen men.' Two hundred thousand prostitutes in the city of New York - well? How many patrons? A million, at the least. They kept on doing business, and enjoying life. I tell you, John, all the unnecessary evils of condition in the old days, were as nothing to the unnecessary evils of our foolish ideas! And ideas can be changed in the twinkling of an eye!

"As to your hoboes and bums, that invalid tramp you instanced - I can settle your mind on that point. I was an invalid tramp, John; a drunkard, a cocaine fiend, a criminal, sick, desperate, as bad as they make them."

"Which brings us back to that 'moral sanitarium' I suppose?"

"Yes. I strayed away from it. I keep forgetting my own case. But it is an excellent one for illustration. I was taken hold of with the strong hand, and given a course of double treatment, deep and thorough. By double treatment I mean physical and mental at once; such a complete overhauling and wise care as enabled my exhausted vitality slowly to reassert itself, and at the same time such strong tender cheerful companionship, such well-devised entertainment, such interesting, irresistible instruction - Why, John - put a tramp into Paradise, and there's some hope of him."

I was about to say that tramps did not deserve Paradise, but as I remembered what this man had been, and saw what he was now, I refrained.

He read my mind at once.

"It's not a question of desert, John. We no longer deal in terms of personal reward or punishment. If I have a bad finger or a bad tooth I save it if I can; not because it deserves it, but because I need it. People who used to be called sinners are now seen to be diseased members of society, and society turns all its regenerative forces on at once. We never used to dream of that flood of power we had at hand - the Regenerative Forces of Society!"

He sat smiling, his fine eyes full of light. "Sometimes we had to amputate," he continued, "especially at first. It is very seldom necessary now."

"You mean you killed the worst people?"

"We killed many hopeless degenerates, insane, idiots, and real perverts, after trying our best powers of cure. But it is really astonishing to see how much can be done with what we used to call criminals, merely by first-class physical treatment. I can remember how strange it seemed to me, having elaborate baths, massage, electric stimulus, perfect food, clean comfortable beds, beautiful clothes, books, music, congenial company, and wonderful instruction. It was very confusing. It went far to rearrange all my ideas."

"If you treat - social invalids - like that, I should think they would 'lie down' just to remain in hospital forever. Or go out and be bad in order to get back again."

"Oh, no," he said. "A healthy man can't lie around and do nothing very long. Also it is good outside too, remember. Life is good, pleasant, easy. Why on earth should a man want to prowl around at night and steal when he can have all he wants, with less effort, in the daytime? Happy people do not become criminals.

"But I can tell you what treatment like that does to one. It gives a man a new view of human life, of what it is he belongs to. A sense of pride in our common accomplishment, of gratitude for the pleasure he receives, of a natural desire to contribute something. I took this new ethics - it satisfied me, it's reasonable, it's necessary. We make it our basic study now, in all the schools. You must have noticed that?"

"Yes, I had noticed it, as I looked back. But they don't call it that," I said.

"No, they don't call it anything to the children. It is just life, the rules of decent behavior."

We sat silent awhile after this. Things were clearing up a little in my mind.

"A sort of crystallization of chaotic progressive thought into clear diamonds of usable truth - is that about what happened?" I said.

"That's exactly it,"

"And a general refutation and clearing out of - of - "

"Of a lot of things we deeply believed - that were not so! That is what was the matter with us, John. Our minds were full of what Mrs. Eddy christened error. I wish I could make you feel what a sunrise it was to the world when we left off believing lies and learned the facts."

"Can you, in a few words, outline a little of your new 'Ethics' to the lay mind?"

"Easily. It is all 'lay' enough. We don't make a separate profession of religion, or a separate science of ethics. Ethics is social hygiene - it teaches how humanity must live in order to be well and strong. We show the child the patent facts of social relation, how all our daily life, our accumulated wealth and beauty and continuing power, rests on common action, on what people do together. Everything about him teaches that. Then we show him the reasons why such and such actions are wrong, what the results are; how to avoid wrong lines of action and adopt right ones. It's no more difficult than teaching any other game, and far more interesting."

I suppose I looked unconvinced, for he added, "Remember we have nature on our side. It is natural for a social animal to develop social instincts; any personal desire which works against the social good is clearly a survival of a lower presocial period; wrong, in that it is out of place. What we used to call criminals were relics of the past. By artificially maintaining low conditions, such as poverty, individual wealth, we bred low-grade types. We do not breed them any more."

Again we sat silent. I was nursing my knee and sat looking into the fire; the soft shimmering play of rosy light and warmth with which electricity now gave jewels to our rooms.

He followed my eyes.

"That clean, safe, beautiful power was always here, John - but we had not learned of it. The power of wind and water and steam were here - before we learned to use them. All this splendid power of human life was here - only we did not know it."

After that talk with Frank Borderson I felt a little clearer in my mind about what had taken place. I saw a good deal of him, and he introduced me to others who were in his line of work. Also I got to know his wife pretty well. She was not so great an authority on ethics as he; but an excellent teacher, widely useful.

One day I said something to her about her lovely spirit, and what she must have been to him - such an uplifting influence.

She laughed outright.

"I'll have to tell you the facts, Mr. Robertson, as part of your instruction. So far from my uplifting him, he picked me out of the gutter, literally, dead drunk in the gutter, the lowest kind of wreck. He made me over. He gave me - Life."

Her eyes shone.

"We work together," she added cheerfully.

They did work together, and evidently knew much happiness. I noted a sort of deep close understanding between them, as in those who have been through the wars in company,

I found Nellie knew about them. "Yes, indeed," she said. "They are devoted to each other, and most united in their work. He was just beginning to try to work, after his own rebuilding; but feeling pretty lonesome. He felt that he had no chance of any personal life, you see, and there were times when he missed it badly. He had no right to marry, of course; that is, with a well woman. And then he found this broken lily - and mended it. There can't be any children, but there is great happiness, you can see that."

"And they are - received?"

"Received? - Oh, I remember. You mean they are invited to dinners and parties. Why, yes."

"Not among the best people, surely?"

"Precisely that, the very best; people who appreciate their wonderful lives."

"Tell me this, Sister; what happened to the Four Hundred - the F. F. V's - and the rest of the aristocracy?"

"The same thing that happened to all of us. They were only people, you see. Their atrophied social consciousness was electrified with the new thoughts and feelings. They woke up, too, most of them. Some just died out harmlessly. They were only by-products."

I consulted a rather reactionary old professor of Sociology, Morris Banks; one who had been teaching Political Economy in my youth, and who ought to be able to remember things. I asked him if he would be so good as to show me the dark side of this shield.

"Surely there must have been opposition, misunderstanding, the usual difficulties of new adjustments," I said. "You remember the first years of change - I wish you would give me a clear account of it."

The old man considered awhile: "Take any one state, any city, or country locality, and study back a little," he said, "and you find the story is about the same. There was opposition and dissent, of course, but it decreased very rapidly. You see the improvements at first introduced were such universal benefits that there could not be any serious complaint.

"By the time we had universal suffrage the women were more than ready for it, full of working plans to carry out, and rich by the experience of the first trials.

"By the time Socialism was generally adopted we had case after case of proven good in Socialistic methods; and also the instructive background of some failures."

"But the big men who ran the country to suit themselves in my time, they didn't give up without a struggle surely? You must have had *some* fighting," I said.

He smiled in cheerful reminiscence. "We had a good deal of noise, if that's what you mean. But there's no fighting to be done, with soldiers, if the soldiers won't fight. Our workingmen declined to shoot or to be shot any longer, and left the big capitalists to see what they could do alone."

"But they had the capital?"

"Not all of it. The revenues of the cities and of the United States Government are pretty considerable, especially when you save the seventy per cent we used to spend on wars past and possible; and the ten or twenty more that went in waste and graft. With a Socialist State private Capital has no grip!"

"Did you confiscate it?"

"Did not have to. The people who were worth anything, swung into line and went to work like other people. Those that weren't were just let alone. Nobody has any respect for them now."

"You achieved Socialism without blood-shed?"

"We did. It did not happen all at once, you see; just spread and spread and proved its usefulness."

CHAPTER 12

More and more I cut loose from the explanatory guiding strings of my sister and the family, even from the requested information of specialists, and wandered by myself in search of the widening daily acquaintance which alone could make life seem real again.

It was an easy world to wander in. The standard of general courtesy and intelligence of the officials, and of the average passer-by, was as much above what I remembered as the standard in Boston used to be above that of New York.

As most of the business was public business one could study and inquire freely. As much work as could be advantageously localized was so arranged, this saving in transportation. The clothing industry, for in stance, instead of being carried on in swarming centers, and then distributed all over the country, formed part of the pleasant everyday work in each community and was mostly in the hands of women.

As a man I could appreciate little of the improved quality of fabrics, save as I noticed their beauty, and that my own clothes wore longer, and both looked and felt more agreeable. But women told me how satisfying it was to know that silk was silk, and wool, wool. This improvement in textile values, with the outgrowing of that long obsession called fashion, reduced the labor of clothes-making materially.

Women's clothes, I found, as I strolled were very delicate and fine, and had a gracious dignity and sanity far removed from the frantic concoctions I remembered in the windows; - shredded patchwork of muslin and lace, necessarily frail and short-lived even as ornaments, never useful, and costing arduous labor in construction, with corresponding expense to the purchaser.

The robes and gowns were a joy to the eye. Some showed less taste than others, naturally, but nowhere was to be seen the shameless ugliness so common in my youth.

Beauty and peace, I found, care, leisure, quietness, plenty of gaiety, too, both in young and old. It struck me that the young people, owing to their wider and sounder upbringing, were more serious, and that older people, owing to their safer, easier lives, were jollier. These sweet-faced, broad-minded young women did not show so much giggling inanity as once seemed necessary to them; and a young man, even a young man in college, did not, therefore, find pleasure in theft, cruelty, gross practical jokes and destruction of property.

As I noted this, I brought myself up with a start. It looked as if Nellie had written it. Surely, when I was in college - and there rose up within me a memory of the crass, wasteful follies that used to be called "pranks" in my time, and considered perfectly natural in young men. I had not minded them in those days. It gave me a queer feeling to see by my own words how my judgment was affected already.

I explored the city from end to end, and satisfied myself that there was no poverty in it, no street that was not clean, no house that was not fit for human habitation. That is, as far as I could judge from an outside view.

Among the masses of people, after their busy mornings, there were vast numbers who used the afternoons for learning, the easy, interesting, endless learning now carried on far and wide. The more they learned the more they wanted to know; and the best minds, free for research work, and upheld in it by the deepening attention of the world, constantly pushed on the boundaries of knowledge.

There were some hospitals yet, but as one to a hundred of what used to be, of higher quality, and fuller usefulness. There were some of what I should have called prisons, though the life inside was not only as comfortable as that without, but administered with a stricter care for the advantage of those within.

There were the moral sanitariums - healthful and beautiful, richly endowed with the world's best methods of improvement, and managed by the world's best people. It made me almost dizzy to try to take in this opposite pole of judgment on the criminal.

Out of town I found that the park-like roads, so generally in use, by no means interfered with the wide stretches of what I used to call "real country." Intensive agriculture took less ground, rather more; and the wide use of food-bearing trees had restored the wooded aspect, so pleasant in every sense.

The small country towns were of special interest to me; I visited scores of them; each differing from the others, all beautiful and clean and busy. They were numerous too; replacing the areas of scattered lonely farmhouses, with these comfortable and pretty groups, each in its home park, with its standard of convenience as high as that in any town.

The smallest group had its power plant, supplying all the houses with heat, light and water, had its child gardens, its Town House and Club House, its workshops and foodshops as necessary as its post offices.

The Socialized industries ensured employment to every citizen, and provided all the necessaries of life - larger order this than it used to be. Quite above this broad base of social control, the life of the people went on; far freer and more open to individual development than it had ever had a chance to be in the whole history of the world.

This I frankly conceded. I found I was making more concessions in my note-book than I had yet made to either Nellie or Owen. They encouraged me to travel about by myself. In fact, my sister was now about to resume her college position and Owen was going with her.

They both advised me not to settle upon any work for a full year.

"That's little enough time in which to cover thirty," Nellie said, patting my shoulder. "But you're doing splendidly, John. We are proud of you. And there's no hurry. You know there's enough from our mine to enable you to join the 'leisure class' - if you want to!"

I had no idea of doing this, as she well knew, but I did feel it necessary to get myself in some way grafted on to this new world before I took up regular employment. I found that there was not much call for ancient languages in the colleges, even if I had been in touch with the new methods; but there remained plenty of historical work, for which I had now a special fitness. Indeed some of my new scientific friends assured me I could be of the utmost service, with my unique experience.

So I was not worried about what to do, nor under any pressure about doing it. But the more I saw of all these new advantages, the more I was obliged to admit that they were advantages; the more I traveled and read and learned, the more lonesome and homesick I became.

It was a beautiful world, but it was not my world. It was like a beautiful dream, but seemed a dream nevertheless. I could no longer dispute that it was possible for people to be "healthy, wealthy and wise"; and happy, too - visibly happy - here they all were; working and playing and enjoying life as naturally as possible. But they were not the people I used to know; those, too, were like Frank Borderson and Morris Banks - changed so that they seemed more unreal than the others.

The beauty and peace and order of the whole thing wore on me. I wanted to hear the roar of the elevated trains - to smell the foul air of the subway and see the people pile in, pushing and angry, as I still remembered in my visits to New York.

I wanted to see some neglected-looking land, some ragged suburbs, some far-away farmhouse alone under its big elms, with its own barns in odorous proximity, its own cows, boy-driven, running and stumbling home to be milked.

I wanted a newspaper which gave me the excitement of guessing what the truth was, I wanted to see some foolish, crazily dressed, giggling girls, and equally foolish boys, but better dressed and less giggling, given to cigarettes and uproarious "good times."

I was homesick, desperately homesick. So without saying a word to anyone I betook myself to old Slide-face, to see Uncle Jake.

All the way down - and I went by rail - no air travel for this homecoming! - I felt an increasing pleasure in the familiar look of things. The outlines of the Alleghanies had not changed. I would not get out at any town, the shining neatness of the railroad station was enough; but the sleeping cars were a disappointment. The beds were wide, soft, cool, the blankets of light clean wool, the air clear and fresh, the noise and jar almost gone. Oh, well, I couldn't expect to have everything as it used to be, of course.

But when I struck out, on foot, from Paintertown, and began to climb the road that led to my old home, my heart was in my mouth. It was a better road, of course - but I hardly noticed that. All the outlying farms were better managed and the little village groups showed here and there - but I shut my eyes to these things.

The hills were the same - the hills I had grown up among. They couldn't alter the face of the earth much - that was still recognizable. Our own house I did not visit - both father and mother were gone, and the little wooden building replaced by a concrete mining office. Nellie had told me about all this; it was one reason why I had not come back before.

But now I went past our place almost with my eyes shut; and kept on along the road to Uncle Jake's. He had been a rich man, as farmers went, owning the land for a mile or two on every side, owning Slide-face as a matter of fact; and as he made enough from the rich little upland valley where the house stood, to pay his taxes, he owned it still.

The moment I reached his boundary I knew it, unmistakably. A ragged, home-made sign, sagging from its nails, announced "Private Road. No trespassers allowed." Evidently they heeded the warning, for the stony, washed-out roadbed was little traveled.

My heart quite leaped as I set foot on it. It was not "improved" in the least from what I remembered in my infrequent visits. My father and Uncle Jake had "a coldness" between them; which would have been a quarrel, I fancy, if father had not been a minister, so I never saw much of these relations.

Drusilla I remembered well enough, though, a pretty, babyish thing, and Aunt Dorcas's kind, patient, tired smile, and the fruit cakes she made.

Up and up, through the real woods, ragged and thick with dead boughs, fallen trunks and underbrush, not touched by any forester, and finally, around the shoulder of Slide-face, to the farm.

I stood still and drew in a long breath of utter satisfaction. Here was something that had not changed. There was an old negro plowing, the same negro I remembered, apparently not a day older. It is wonderful how little they do change with years. His wool showed white though, as he doffed his ragged cap and greeted me with cheerful cordiality as Mass' John.

"We all been hearin' about you, Mass' John. We been powerful sorry 'bout you long time, among de heathen," he said. "You folks'll be glad to see you!"

'Well, young man!" said Uncle Jake, with some show of cordiality; "better late than never. We wondered if you intended to look up your country relations."

But Aunt Dorcas put her thin arms around my neck and kissed me, teary kisses with little pats and exclamations. "To think of it! Thirty years among savages! We heard about it from Nellie - she wrote us, of course. Nellie's real good to keep us posted."

"She never comes to see us!" said my Uncle. "Nor those youngsters of hers. We've never had them here but once. They're too 'advanced' for old-fashioned folks."

Uncle Jake's long upper lip set firmly; I remembered that look, as he used to sit in his wagon and talk with mother &t our gate, refusing to come in, little sunny-haired Drusilla looking shyly at me from under her sunbonnet the while.

Where was Drusilla? Surely not - that! A frail, weak, elderly, quiet, little woman stood there by Aunt Dorcas, her smooth fine, ash-brown hair drawn tightly back to a flat knot behind, her dull blue calico dress falling starkly about her.

She came forward, smiling, and held out a thin work-worn hand. "We're so glad to see you, Cousin John," she said. "We certainly are."

They made much of me in the old familiar ways I had so thirsted for. The sense of family background, of common knowledge and experience was comforting in the extreme, the very furnishings and clothes as I recalled them. I told them what a joy it was.

This seemed to please Uncle Jake enormously.

"I *thought* you'd do it," he said. "Like to find one place that hasn't been turned upside down by all these new-fangled notions. Dreadful things have been goin' on, John, while you were amongst them Feejees."

I endeavored to explain to him something of the nature and appearance of the inhabitants of Tibet, but it made small impression. Uncle Jake's mind was so completely occupied by what was in it, that any outside fact or idea had small chance of entry.

"They've got wimmin votin' now, I understand," he pursued; "I don't read the papers much, they are so ungodly, but I've heard that. And they've been meddlin' with Divine Providence in more ways than one - but I keep out of it, and so does Aunt Dorcas and the girl here."

He looked around at my Aunt, who smiled her gentle, faithful smile, and at Drusilla, who dropped her eyes and flushed faintly. I suspected her of secret leanings toward the movement of the world outside.

"I don't allow my family off the farm," he went on, "except when we go to meetin', and that's not often. There's hardly an orthodox preacher left, seems to me; but we go up to the Ridge meetin' house sometimes."

"I should think you would find it a little dull - don't you?" I ventured.

Drusilla flashed a grateful look at me.

"Nothing of the sort," he answered. "I was born on this farm, and it's big enough for anybody to be contented on. Your Aunt was born over in Hadley Holler - and she's contented enough. As for Drusilly - " he looked at her again with real affection, "Drusilly 's always been a good girl - never made any trouble in her life. Unless 'twas when she pretty near married that heretic minister - eh, Drusilly?"

My cousin did not respond warmly to this sally, but neither did she show signs of grief. I was conscious of a faint satisfaction that she had not married the heretic minister.

They made me very welcome, so welcome indeed that as days passed, Uncle Jake even broached the subject of my remaining there.

"I've got no son," he said, "and a girl can't run the farm. You stay here, John, and keep things goin', and I'll will it to you - what do you say? You ain't married, I see. Just get you a nice girl - if there's any left, and settle down here."

I thanked him warmly, but said I must have time to consider - that I had thought of accepting other work which offered.

He was most insistent about it. "You better stay here, John. Here's pure air and pure food - none of these artificial kickshaws I hear of folks havin' nowadays. We smoke our own hams just as we used to do in my grandfather's time - there's none better. We buy sugar and rice and coffee and such as that; but I grind my own corn in the little mill there on the creek - reckon I'm the only one who uses it now. And your Aunt runs her loom to this day. Drusilly can, too, but she 'lows she hates to do it. Girls aren't what they used to be when I was young!"

It did not seem possible that Uncle Jake had ever been young. His sturdy, stooping frame, his hard, ruddy features were the same at seventy as I remembered them at forty, only the hair, whitened and thinned, was different.

My bedroom was exactly as when I last slept in it, on my one visit to the farm as a boy of fifteen. Drusilla had seemed only a baby then - a slender little five-year old. She had followed me about in silence, with adoring eyes, and I had teased her! - I hated to think of how I had teased her.

The gold in her hair was all dulled and faded, the rose-leaf color of her cheeks had faded, too, and her blue eyes wore a look of weary patience. She worked hard. Her mother was evidently feeble now, and the labor required in that primitive home was considerable.

The old negro brought water from the spring and milked the cows, but all the care of the dairy, the cooking for the family, the knitting and sewing and mending and the sweeping, scrubbing and washing was in the hands of Aunt Dorcas and Drusilla.

She would make her mother sit down and chat with me, while Uncle Jake smoked his cob pipe, but she herself seemed always at work.

"There's no getting any help nowadays," said my Uncle. "Even if we needed it. Old Joe there stayed on - he was here before I was born. Joe must be eighty or over - there's no telling the age of niggers. But the young ones are too uppity for any use. They want to be paid out of all reason, and treated like white folks at that!"

He boasted that he had never worn a shirt or a pair of socks made off the place. "In my father's time we raised a heap of cotton and sold it. Plenty of niggers then. Now I manage to get enough for my own use, and we spin and weave it on the spot!"

I watched Aunt Dorcas at her wheel and loom, and rubbed my eyes. It was only in the remote mountain regions that these things were done when I was young, and to see it now seemed utterly incredible. But Uncle Jake was proud of it.

"I don't believe there's another wheel agoin' in the whole country," he said. "The mountains ain't what they used to be, John. They've got the trees all grafted up with new kinds of foolishness - nuts and fruit and one thing'n another - and unheard-of kinds of houses and schools, and play-acting everywhere. I can't abide it,"

He set his jaw firmly, making the stiff white beard stand out at a sharp angle. "The farm'll keep us for my time," he concluded; "but I should hate to have it all 'reformed' and torn to pieces after I'm gone." And he looked meaningly at me.

I lingered on, still enjoying the sense of family affection, but my satisfaction in the things about me slowly cooling.

A cotton quilt was heavier but not so warm as a woolen blanket. Homespun sheets were durable, doubtless, but not comfortable. The bathing to be done in a small steep-sided china basin, with water poured from a pitcher the outlines of which were more concave than convex, was laborious and unsatisfying.

The relish of that "hog and hominy" and the beaten biscuit, the corn pone, the molasses and pork gravy of my youth, wore off as the same viands reappeared on the table from day to day and week to week, and seemed ceaselessly present within me.

It was pleasant to listen to Aunt Dorcas's gentle reminiscences of the past years, of my father and mother in their youth, of my infancy, and Drusilla's. She grieved that she had not more to tell. "I never was one to visit much," she said.

But it was saddening to find that the dear old lady could talk of absolutely nothing else. In all her sixty-eight years she had known nothing else; her father's home and her husband's, alike in their contents and in their labors, her own domestic limitations, and those of her neighbors, and her church paper - taken for forty years, and arbitrarily discontinued by Uncle Jake because it had grown too liberal.

"It never seemed over-liberal to me," she said softly, "and I do miss it. I wouldn't a'believed I'd a'missed anything so much. It used to come every week, and I kept more acquainted with what the rest of this circuit was doing. But your Uncle Jake is so set against liberalism!"

I turned to my cousin for some wider exchange of thoughts, and strove with all the remembered arts of my youth, and all the recently acquired wisdom of my present years, to win her confidence.

It was difficult at first. She was shy with the dumb shyness of an animal; not like a wild animal, frankly curious, not like a hunted animal, which runs away and hides, but like an animal in a menagerie, a sullen, hopeless timidity, due to long restriction. Life had slipped by her, all of it, as far as she knew. She had been an "old maid" for twenty-five years - they call them that in these mountains if they are not married at twenty. Her father's domineering ways had discouraged most of the few young men she had known, and he had ruthlessly driven away the only one who came near enough to be dismissed.

Then it was only the housework, and caring for her mother as she grew older. The one pleasure of her own she ever had was in her flowers. She had transplanted wild ones, had now and then been given "a slip" by remote neighbors - in past years; and those carefully nurtured blossoms were all that brought color and sweetness into her gray life.

She did not complain. For a long time I could not get her to talk to me at all about herself, and when she did it was without hope or protest. She had practically no education - only a few years in a country school in childhood, and almost no reading, writing, conversation, any sort of knowledge of the life of the world about her.

And here she lived, meek, patient, helpless, with neither complaint nor desire, endlessly working to make comfortable the parents who must some day leave her alone - to what?

My thirty years in Tibet seemed all at once a holiday compared to this thirty years on an upland farm in the Alleghanies of Carolina. My loss of life - what was it to this loss? I, at least, had never known it, not until I was found and brought back, and she had known it every day and night for thirty years. I had come back at fifty-five, regaining a new youth in a new world. She apparently had had no youth, and now was old - older at forty-five than women of fifty and sixty whom I had met and talked with recently.

I thought of them, those busy, vigorous, eager, active women, of whom no one would ever predicate either youth or age; they were just women, permanently, as men were men. I thought of their wide, free lives, their absorbing work and many minor interests, and the big, smooth, beautiful, moving world in which they lived, and my heart went out to Drusilla as to a baby in a well.

"Look here, Drusilla," I said to her at last, "I want you to marry me. We'll go away from here; you shall see something of life, my dear - there's lot of time yet."

She raised those quiet blue eyes and looked at me, a long, sweet, searching look, and then shook her head with gentle finality. "O, no," she said. "Thank you, Cousin John, but I could not do that."

And then, all at once I felt more lonely and out of life than when the first shock met me.

"O, Drusilla!" I begged; "Do - do! Don't you see, if you won't have me nobody ever will? I am all alone in the world, Drusilla; the world has all gone away from me! You are the only woman alive who would understand. Dear cousin - dear little girl - you'll have to marry me - out of pity!" And she did.

· · · · ·

Nobody would know Drusilla now. She grew young at a rate that seemed a heavenly miracle. To her the world was like heaven, and, being an angel was natural to her anyway.

I grew to find the world like heaven, too - if only for what it did to Drusilla.

finis

THE HERLAND TRILOGY

Charlotte Perkins Gilman was an American sociologist, poet, novelist, and activist for gender equality and social reform. Her most famous work today is the semi-autobiographical, *The Yellow Wallpaper*, (also published by Aziloth Books), but arguably more important is Gilman's fictional 'Herland Trilogy'. Universally recognized as a classic of early feminist literature, the books recount the utopian advances made in 'Herland' - a parthenogenetic all-female society isolated from the rest of humanity for 2000 years - and the disruption caused by the arrival of three male American adventurers.

Moving The Mountain

Moving the Mountain was published in Gilman's magazine *The Forerunner* in 1911, and appeared in book form later that same year. It tells the tale of American John Robertson, a native of South Carolina, and student of ancient languages, who at the age of 25 travels to Tibet and, after an unfortunate accident, suffers complete memory loss. Thirty years later, in 1940, he is found by his sister Nellie, recovers his memory and returns to the United States.

Much has altered since John left his native shore. Women have become emancipated and have changed many aspects of society for the better: crime, poverty, prostitution, corruption and racism are no more. For John the culture shock is extreme – he retains the misogynist world-view of his youth, and finds equality of the sexes a bitter pill to swallow. Gilman skillfully uses John's (fictional) reactionary feelings to dissect and reject the (actual) domination and gender discrimination practiced by the men of her own time. A timely reminder of how far feminism has come – and altered - in the past 100 years.

Herland

Charlotte Perkins Gilman was known as a crusading feminist intellectual, concerned especially with gender inequality within marriage. Most married women of her time had little chance of participating in any creative or professional career – an enforced domestic slavery that was, for Gilman, not only patently unjust, but made neither partner happy or content.

In *Herland*, Gilman weaves these themes into an adventure story of three young men, schooled in the then-current view of women as weak and timid creatures. They discover Herland, an all-female society of rationality, equality and compassion composed solely of strong, athletic women, where even reproduction requires no male input. Gilman uses this utopian fantasy with skill and humour, gradually bringing the three male adventurers from an initial arrogant confidence in their own culture, to a realization that life in Herland is infinitely preferable to the war-torn, poverty-stricken male-dominated nations they have left. And that the supposed inferiority of the weaker sex is, in fact, nothing more than a product of cultural indoctrination.

With Her In Ourland

With Her in Ourland is the third and final installment of the saga, and has Herlander Ellador, now married (platonically) to Vandyck Jennings, leaving her home and engaging in a tour of 'Ourland' - the rest of the world. Ellador's calm, logical responses to the problems of war, poverty, misogyny, racial prejudice and other worldly evils, allow Gilman to continue her satirical, dystopian critique of the so-called civilized world, with husband Vandyck's complacent acceptance of worldly injustice acting as the perfect foil to Ellador/Gilman's prescriptions for setting the place to rights. The result is a *tour de force* of Charlotte Gilman's wit and political perception, making for an astute and distinctly prescient account of both our past, and present-day, problems.

AZILOTH ||| BOOKS

Aziloth Books publishes a wide range of titles ranging from hard-to-find esoteric books - Parchment Books - to classic works on fiction, politics and philosophy - Cathedral Classics. Our newest venture is Aziloth Books Children's Classics, with vibrant new covers and Black-and-White/Colour illustrations to complement some of the world's very best children's tales. All our imprints are offered to the reader at a competitive price and through as many mediums and outlets as possible.

We are committed to excellent book production and strive, whenever possible, to add value to our titles with original images, maps and author introductions. With the premium on space in most modern dwellings, we also endeavour - within the limits of good book design - to make our products as slender as possible, allowing more books to be fitted into a given bookshelf area.

We are a small, approachable company and would love to hear any of your comments and suggestions on our plans, products, or indeed on absolutely anything.

Aziloth Books is also interested in hearing from aspiring authors whom we might publish. We look forward to meeting you.

Contact us at: info@azilothbooks.com.

CATHEDRAL CLASSICS

Cathedral Classics hosts an array of classic literature, from erudite ancient tomes to avant-garde, twentieth-century masterpieces, all of which deserve a place in your home. All the world's great novelists are here, Jane Austen, Dickens, Conrad, Arthur Machen and Henry James, brushing shoulders with such disparate luminaries as Sun Tzu, Marcus Aurelius, Kipling, Friedrich Nietzsche, Machiavelli, and Omar Khayam. A small selection is detailed below:

Frankenstein	Mary Shelley
The Time Machine; The Invisible Man	H. G. Wells
The Prince	Niccolo Machiavelli
The Rubaiyat of Omar Khayyam	Omar Khayyam
Heart of Darkness; The Secret Agent	Joseph Conrad
Persuasion; Northanger Abbey	Jane Austen
The Picture of Dorian Gray	Oscar Wilde
Candide	Voltaire
The Coming Race	Bulwer Lytton
The Adventures of Sherlock Holmes	Arthur Conan Doyle
The Thirty-Nine Steps	John Buchan
Beyond Good and Evil	Friedrich Nietzsche
Washington Square	Henry James
The Red Badge of Courage	Stephen Crane
Self-Reliance, & Other Essays (series1&2)	Ralph W. Emmerson
The Art of War	Sun Tzu
A Christmas Carol	Charles Dickens
The Gambler; The Double	Fyodor Dostoyevsky
To the Lighthouse; Mrs Dalloway	Virginia Woolf
The Sorrows of Young Werther	Johann W. Goethe
Leaves of Grass - 1855 edition	Walt Whitman
Analects	Confucius
Beowulf	Anonymous
Agnes Grey	Anne Bronte
Utopia	Thomas More

Obtainable at all good online and local bookstores.
View Aziloth Books' full list at: www.azilothbooks.com

PARCHMENT BOOKS

Parchment Books enshrines the concept of the oneness of all true religious traditions - that "the light shines from many different lanterns". Our list below offers titles from both eastern and western spiritual traditions, including Christian, Judaic, Islamic, Daoist, Hindu and Buddhist mystical texts, as well as books on alchemy, hermeticism, paganism, etc..

By bringing together such spiritual texts, we hope to make esoteric and occult knowledge more readily available to those ready to receive it. We do not publish grimoires or any titles pertaining to the left hand path. Titles include:

Abandonment to Divine Providence	Jean-Pierre de Caussade
Corpus Hermeticum	G.R.S. Mead (trans.)
The Holy Rule of St Benedict	St. Benedict of Nursia
Kundalini	G. S. Arundale
The Way of Perfection	St. Teresa of Avila
Q.B.L.	Frater Achad
The Cloud Upon the Sanctuary	Karl von Eckhartshausen
The Confession of St Patrick	St. Patrick
The Outline of Sanity	G K Chesterton
The Teachings of Zoroaster	Shapuji A Kapadia
The Dialogue Of St Catherine Of Siena	St. Catherine of Siena
Esoteric Christianity	Annie Besant
The Wisdom of the Egyptians	Brian Brown
The Spiritual Exercises of St. Ignatius	St. Ignatius of Loyola
Dark Night of the Soul	St. John of the Cross
Moses and Monotheism	Sigmund Freud
The Gospel of Thomas	Anonymous
Alchemy Rediscovered and Restored	Archibald Cockren
The Imitation of Christ	Thomas à Kempis
The Interior Castle	St. Teresa of Avila
Songs of Innocence & Experience	William Blake
The Marriage of Heaven & Hell	William Blake
The Secret of the Rosary	St. Louis de Montfort
Tertium Organum	P.D. Ouspensky
From Ritual to Romance	Jessie L. Weston
The God of the Witches	Margaret Murray

Obtainable at all good online and local bookstores.
View Aziloth Books' full list at: www.azilothbooks.com

AZILOTH BOOKS CHILDREN'S CLASSICS

Aziloth Books is passionate about bringing the very best in children's classics fiction to the next generation of book-lovers. Renowned for its original design and outstanding quality, our highly successful list has something to suit every age and interest. Titles include:

The Railway Children	Edith Nesbit
5 Children and It	Edith Nesbit
Anne of Green Gables	Lucy Maud Montgomery
What Katy Did	Susan Coolidge
What Katy Did Next	Susan Coolidge
Puck of Pook's Hill	Rudyard Kipling
The Jungle Books	Rudyard Kipling
Just So Stories	Rudyard Kipling
Alice Through the Looking Glass	Charles Dodgson
Alice's Adventures in Wonderland	Charles Dodgson
Black Beauty	Anna Sewell
The War of the Worlds	H. G Wells
The Time Machine	H. G .Wells
The Sleeper Awakes	H. G. Wells
The Invisible Man	H. G. Wells
The Lost World	Sir Arthur Conan Doyle
A Christmas Carol	Charles Dickens
Call of the Wild	Jack London
Greenmantle	John Buchan
Treasure Island	Robert Louis Stevenson
Dr Jekyll and Mr Hyde	Robert Louis Stevenson
Kidnapped	Robert Louis Stevenson
Catriona (David Balfour)	Robert Louis Stevenson
The Water Babies	Charles Kingsley
The First Men in the Moon	Jules Verne
The Secret Garden	Frances Hodgson Burnett
A Little Princess	Frances Hodgson Burnett
Peter Pan	J. M. Barrie

Obtainable at all good online and local bookstores.
View Aziloth Books' full list at: www.azilothbooks.com